A KILLER AT THE CASTLE

KELLY MASON

LITTLE ORCHARD PRESS

For Diana, Ellen and Phoebe <3 xxx

CHAPTER 1

"*I*t's jolly nice to take breakfast without discussing death," Captain Ernest Hamilton said as he sat with myself and Miss Lottie Penny in the Seaview Restaurant at Millar's. The hotel had been built on an elevated position with beautiful views over the seaside resort of Branden Bay. The bay sported a beautiful horseshoe of yellow sand with a pier jutting out to sea, where boats from Bristol and Wales brought day trippers who took advantage of the fairground or stayed for a night or longer to unwind in the many jazz and cocktail bars.

"I could not agree more," I said as I studied the food spread out before us. I noticed that certain items, such as the sliced fruit and more exotic conserves, were missing from the usual breakfast menu. Since the hotel owner, Mr James Millar, had returned with his wife and nephew from a long trip to India, there had been

1

certain cutbacks. Not that I blamed him. When they had left Branden Bay for their trip to India, Millar's Hotel was fully booked for months ahead. Upon their return they found that the hotel was only half filled, with many future bookings also cancelled. Those that chose to remain at the hotel often forwent the hotel food after a man had died face down in his soup in the very restaurant in which we were seated. The victim, Major Coltrane, had been a most disagreeable man and I had been dragged into the investigation following an argument with the major moments before his death. This had led to me being placed at the top of the suspect list in Scotland Yard's hunt for a murderer.

"I really miss our investigation," Lottie said in her London accent. She often tried to mask her class by ensuring she sounded the ending of her words. I found this rather endearing. Whilst I had employed her as my assistant, over the weeks we'd spent together at the hotel I'd become rather fond of her, in a sisterly way. I admired Lottie's youthful outlook and her desire for social mobility. But as far as her thirst for more excitement was concerned, I was rather happy that over the preceding week our lives had become much more sedate.

"Investigating was really exhilarating," Lottie said. "The last few weeks have been the best of my whole life." She beamed at me. Lottie was seventeen and still carried the inquisitive qualities of a child.

"If you miss it that much," Hamilton said, "you could always move on to the City of Bristol." He showed Lottie the newspaper. "The Vigilante Slasher has been at work again."

"Oh dear," I said with a frown. "Who died this time?"

"Some chap called Donny Fingo," Hamilton said. "He was a crime lord and smuggler working as part of a duo with his twin brother Larry. The Slasher picks out the criminals that escape the strong arm of the law, hence the tag 'vigilante'."

"Two wrongs don't make a right," I said, sounding very much like my childhood nanny.

At that moment my dog, Prince, stood up and leaned back on his haunches as he gave a long stretch. He had been sleeping next to my chair following the long early morning walk which Lottie had taken him on. He was an Irish Setter that I had rescued as a pup. Being the runt of the litter, he was about to be destroyed by my gamekeeper when I intervened. But despite his weak start, Prince had grown into a strong and healthy dog – and a faithful companion to me.

"You can't go around killing people because of the bad things they've done," I said as Prince sat, gazing up at me for a treat.

"I reckon he just likes knocking people off and picks on bad ones so he doesn't feel so bad about it," Lottie said.

"Personally, I think he does the job the police find themselves powerless to do," Hamilton said. "These crime lords slip under the radar."

Lottie lowered her voice. "How does he kill them?"

she asked as if she didn't really want to know the answer.

"All sorts of ways," I said. "But they know it was him as he slashes a cross on the inside of his victim's left arm." I'd read about the Slasher myself some months before.

"That's disgusting." Lottie scrunched up her face.

"And he takes a trophy," Hamilton added.

"Like what? An ear?" she asked, rubbing her left lobe.

Hamilton laughed. "No, an item the person is associated with. For instance, he took Donny Fingo's pipe. The man was never without it." Hamilton folded the newspaper and placed it on the table beside him before reaching for a slice of toast.

"I hope Sebastian will be safe in Bristol," Lottie said. She was referring to her childhood sweetheart who was staying with family for the summer at Gosford Hall, just outside the city. Sebastian and his cousin were due to join Oxford University. Sebastian, also known as The Earl of Garthorn, was joining us for the day. Lottie had fallen in love with him whilst in service at his family home. Unsurprisingly, his parents, the Marquis and Marchioness of Bandberry, had banished Lottie from their house in Mayfair, which was why she was living on the other side of the country on England's south-west coast. As excited as Lottie was about seeing Sebastian again, I did not hold out much hope for a long-term relationship between the pair, considering the gulf which existed between their positions in society.

Hamilton laughed. "Sebastian is no crime lord. I'm sure the young man will be fine and certainly not on the Slasher's radar."

A waiter brought us fresh pots of tea and coffee.

"Personally, I'm looking forward to a much quieter experience over the remaining summer months," I said. "I'm excited to reacquaint myself with this beautiful town, where I spent many lovely days with my papa."

"When it gets busy, will I have to go back to my duties in the hotel?" Lottie asked as her eyebrows came together in a doleful expression.

I laid my hand upon hers. "You are employed as my assistant and are not a member of the hotel staff anymore. Regardless of whether they continue to speak to you as if you're still working for them." I removed my hand and smiled at her. "I've been telling you for weeks not to be at their beck and call. You're an independent woman."

Lottie sighed. "Mrs Flint is so bossy. I'm glad she's been away this week."

"Don't worry about it, enjoy yourself and help me explore this wonderful seaside town. And there's Prince to keep an eye on." My dog had managed to chew a couple of cushions in my suite, one of which was hand embroidered and had cost me a pretty penny to replace. "And then, assuming you wish to, I would love you to return with me to Ashcombe Hall once the final renovations have been completed."

"Really?" Lottie said. "I thought you only wanted me for three months." She put her hands to her reddening cheeks. "Thank you, Ellen. Thank you so much." Tears sprouted from her eyes. "I'd love to go with you to the hall."

My heart warmed as I watched her dab her eyes with a handkerchief. I'd grown exceptionally close to Lottie and had asked her to call me 'Ellen' a lot less formal than 'My Lady'. I laughed. "When we arrive at Ashcombe, you may regret it. There will be much to be done, you will certainly be earning your wages."

"I'll be the best worker you've ever had." She grinned at me and I was sure she meant it.

"You'll love it there, Lottie," Hamilton said. He had spent time at the hall during the war when it was a convalescent home. I had only recently been reacquainted with Hamilton when we were brought together through the act of clearing our names.

"This is why we must enjoy our time in Branden Bay." I took a sip of my tea.

"I'm guessing it takes a lot to manage the estate," Hamilton said.

I sighed. "If I'm completely honest, I'm not sure what to do with Ashcombe Hall. I have considered how preposterous it is, that a house with so many rooms and so many acres of land is enjoyed by one family." I pulled my fan from the table. "And that family consists of only myself."

"You might marry again and have children," Lottie said then shot a coy look at Hamilton.

I gave myself a strong flutter with my fan. "The responsibility of the hall is enough to keep me occupied." Lottie had been hinting over recent days that she thought Hamilton and myself would make an ideal couple. Since losing my beloved husband during wartime, motherhood was something I thought would never happen to me. I also knew Hamilton would think a relationship with me improper, with us being of different social classes. He had distinct middle-class morals and I was of course the daughter of the late Earl of Ashcombe whilst Hamilton was the son of an accountant.

"What alternative plans do you have for the hall?" Hamilton asked me, thankfully changing the subject to something less personal.

"A school, maybe? Or to open it to the public and turn the gardens into a park."

"They're such beautiful grounds," Hamilton said. "I can picture them in my mind even after nearly six years."

"I can't wait to see the gardens," Lottie said.

"Prince adores his walks there," I said with a smile.

This prompted a woof from my dog, who looked up at me with his wonky but warm brown eyes.

"I'm sure he misses them as he does so love to chase rabbits. But all in good time." The latest letter I had received from the hall notified me that they were some weeks away from completion of the refurbishments. I hoped to oversee the final decoration. I turned to Lottie. "Now – what do you have planned for us today?"

Lottie had taken on the role of planning our sightseeing.

"I've been up to the castle and arranged a private viewing, although Polly in the kitchen was telling me that there have been sightings of a ghost up there."

Hamilton wiped his mouth with his napkin and placed it on the table beside his empty plate. "I wouldn't pay any attention to that nonsense."

"Honestly," Lottie said. "There's this ghost woman who wails about someone being dead as she runs through the tunnels."

I laughed. "You said you wanted something to investigate?"

Lottie frowned. "I hope we don't see anything. I've booked the tour with Mary, she used to work here and is ever so nice." She lowered her voice. "Although there was a bit of a scandal. They say she was having a *close friendship* with Mr Millar and Mrs Millar did not like it, so she sent her packing."

I raised my eyebrows, thinking I would like to know more. I've always been awfully inquisitive although some have referred to me over the years as being nosey.

"I'm honoured that you've invited me along," Hamilton said, closing down the discussion, not being one for idle gossip himself.

"You need some relaxation too," I said to him, "after the events of the last few weeks. When does your next job start?"

"In just over a week. A family who occupy a house in Dulverton, which is close to Exmoor, are holding an event and want security overseen by someone they can trust during the preparations and on the day itself."

"What sort of event is it?" Lottie asked.

"They're having a garden party by invitation only," Hamilton said. "And will have a silent auction for a valuable item."

"Are you sure it's all above board?" I asked.

"The owner assured me it was."

"Can we come?" Lottie asked.

Hamilton laughed. "Unless you are a millionaire with money to spend, it's unlikely you'll receive an invitation."

"I wonder what type of treasure it is?" I asked, feeling my inquisitiveness rise to the surface, then slapped it down. Being nosey did seem to get me into an awful lot of trouble.

"They did not say," Hamilton replied. "But I gather it's a prized item, as they will be paying me very well indeed."

"I'm glad of that, Hamilton," I said. "Considering you lost your last job due to the shenanigans here." Hamilton had been asked not to leave town during the police investigation. "I do wish you had let me pay for your room."

"As generous as you are, Lady Ellen, I have enough put by and am most honoured to be able to accompany yourself and Miss Penny on your exploration of this beautiful seaside resort."

"I do so want to take the boat upriver," I said. "I often watch the steamer bringing passengers in at high tide from my suite balcony."

"I'll book us some tickets on the boat to Bristol," Lottie said. "Well, if you're happy going there with the Slasher!"

I laughed. "I wasn't planning on asking him to join us for luncheon." I turned to Hamilton. "But you are of course invited."

"My lady, I do not wish to impose. I'm already coming with you today to the castle," Hamilton said but his smile said that he very much wanted to spend time with me. That I was sure of.

"You're not in the way," Lottie said to him. "I'm so excited about the trip today."

I raised my eyebrows. "I feel, Lottie, that it is not our company which excites you so, it's the thought of being in the presence of Sebastian."

I gazed out of the window of the Seaview Restaurant. "It's a lovely day for sightseeing. The sky is clear, although it appears to be a little blustery out there." I turned to Lottie. "I hear the views from the castle are mesmerising."

Prince added a woof as if wanting to go outside himself. He had been extremely good sitting beneath the table whilst we ate.

A male voice boomed from the doorway. "Since when have we allowed dogs in the Seaview Restaurant?"

I looked up to see Mr James Millar, the hotel owner,

gesturing at Prince. I had only seen him and his wife from afar and had yet to be formally introduced. Mr Breckon, the hotel manager, had continued with the customer-facing role whilst his employers rested after their travels. Mr Millar was in his mid-thirties and had a fashionable appearance, with slicked back hair, a moustache and a cream suit.

Breckon appeared behind him. The small and stout man's face was crimson. "It was agreed prior to the booking," he said wringing his hands.

"We need words, Breckon – now," James Millar shouted, even though Breckon was not more than a foot away. He about-turned and glared at Breckon before storming off.

"Yes, Mr Millar," Breckon said as he followed him after throwing me an apologetic look. "I just need to make a call from the office."

I rubbed Prince's head and exchanged a glance with Hamilton. "It seems we may not be as welcome as we were before the owner returned."

Lottie bit her lip. "Do you think he saw me? He might not approve of me being in the restaurant either."

I touched her hand. "Calm yourself, how many times do I have to explain this?"

She nodded. "I know, but Mrs Flint's due back today too, she may talk about me to the Millars."

"I wonder how young Joseph is getting along," Hamilton said. Mrs Flint's son had joined a travelling musical show and she had taken time off to watch him in Exeter.

"They might ask us to leave," Lottie said.

"I doubt that will be the case with their dwindling guest list," Hamilton said.

"Lady Ellen." A tall willowy woman with a red curly bob approached me. She wore the hotel's uniform and stretched her hand out towards me. I noticed the gold jewellery around her wrists. This was someone who enjoyed showing off her wealth. "Camilla Millar," she said in a nasal tone.

I felt momentarily stunned. *Camilla Millar, Camilla Millar, Camilla Millar?* Her name echoed in my head. *Would someone really call their child that?* I thought.

"Wife of James Millar, the hotel owner?" she said as if noticing the perplexed look upon my face.

"Ah, indeed," I said, realising, of course, that the unfortunate sounding name had not been handed to her at birth. The parents were forgiven but perhaps she should have considered a double-barrelled alternative when she registered her marriage. I noted also that Camilla appeared to be senior to her husband. She looked mid forties.

"Please excuse my husband, it's been a long and tiring trip back from India and we had rough seas in places. He spent nearly four weeks an awful shade of green."

"And to learn on your return about the death of someone on your property," Hamilton added. "That must have caused stress. But I'm pleased to report that it was Lady Ellen here who solved the mystery."

"Absolutely." She nodded at me. Camilla was being ever so nice and clearly did not want to lose our custom – and rightly so. "I heard all about it from Mr Breckon, even though local gossips seem to think Major Coltrane was killed by salmonella from the chicken soup." She rolled her eyes and sighed.

"That's ridiculous," Hamilton said.

I had to agree because the soup was in fact pea and ham.

"I've never seen it so quiet in here." Camilla looked around the otherwise empty room. "And such a beautiful sunny day." She glanced at me. "We do have many guests here, but few book breakfast. Which is a blessing as the chef has moved on."

I had already heard that the French chef had found employment with their rival 'The Grand Hotel' on the seafront, a traditional style building of the Victorian era and not as modern as the whitewashed façade of Millar's. I had enquired about staying there myself when planning my trip but it was clear from my initial enquiry that they were not at all keen on me bringing Prince. I could not bear to be parted from him for three months.

"I understand the position you're in and I was extremely persuasive when booking in here. I did rather press Mr Breckon to allow me to bring my dog."

"Don't listen to James. Your dog is most welcome."

"And I have employed Lottie to look after Prince full-time so he's not bothersome to other guests."

Camilla smiled at me then frowned at Lottie with

her hand to her chest. "I didn't even recognise you, my dear. You're positively glowing and a woman now." She sighed. "Although that's another staff member we need to replace."

"Lottie has a great amount of intelligence," Hamilton added. "She's an assistant to Lady Ellen as well as minding her dog."

"Well done, Lottie." Camilla turned back to me. "I really do have a lot to catch up on. But I extend my thanks to you for discovering the truth about Major Coltrane's death and clearing the hotel's name."

"Where on earth have the invoices gone?" James Millar's voice floated in from the reception.

Camilla looked towards the door as her husband shouted an obscenity.

Hamilton shook his head. "I say, that's really not on."

Camilla visibly shuddered then turned to us as her cheeks flushed pink. "I am so sorry. Please excuse James, he's worried about the business."

"I completely understand, Mrs Millar," I said. "There's no need to apologise at all."

Hamilton huffed.

"Camilla," James Millar shouted again. He would surely have to change his attitude unless he wanted the hotel to be completely devoid of guests.

"I'd better go," she said and hurried off.

"Dear me," Hamilton said. "I think we should leave, I'm not at all happy with the language considering yourself and Lottie are within hearing distance."

I stood up. "We've finished anyway."

CHAPTER 2

*H*amilton, Lottie and myself were about to take the marble staircase to my suite when our attention was drawn to the reception area.

"Thomas, you don't even know your left from your right!" James Millar bellowed.

We turned around to see both Millars and their nephew, a young man aged twenty, at the reception desk.

"Uncle James," Thomas said. "I thought the receipts were filed in that drawer." He gestured to his left.

"It's not a receipt it's an invoice that needs to be paid and they go in the right. If we leave that one unpaid we'll get a bad reputation."

Thomas frowned. "But Camilla–"

"It's not time for passing the blame," Camilla said. "We need to pull together to get our business back on track. And James, please lower your voice." She glanced over at us. "Don't forget we may not be fully booked but we still have guests." She shook her head, clearly attempting to pacify her husband. "Thomas has a little to learn."

"A little?" James gave a forced laugh as he turned to his nephew. "You've not worked a full day in your entire life!"

"I'm just doing what I'm told." Thomas stared at his aunt.

"We need to buck our ideas up as The Grand has stolen our crown of 'Best Hotel in Branden Bay'. They're fully booked," Camilla said.

"Is that what Angus Scott told you when you met up with him for your little get together?" James Millar asked, his voice laden with accusation.

"James, don't start that again. I've already told you it was nothing of the sort. You can't bring Angus up every time we have a row."

"This is not a row," he shouted.

I baulked, believing that a row certainly described what I was witnessing.

Prince barked and this time all three of the family stared at us.

"And why is that dog still here?" James Millar bellowed as he gestured at Prince.

I turned to Lottie and spoke in a low voice. "Do you want to take Prince into the gardens?"

"Of course," she said and led Prince away as he wagged his tail, eager to get outside having sat so quietly for an hour.

Hamilton whispered to me. "I think maybe we should leave them to their troubles."

I remained rooted to the spot realising it would certainly be polite to walk away. However, I also felt the urge to observe the dynamics at play as the hotel owner and his family team went back to their discussion.

"I don't understand why Ina, who has never taken leave, suddenly needed an entire week off," James Millar said. "Just when we need her the most!"

"I already told you, she's watching Joseph play the piano," Camilla said in answer to her husband.

"I heard the chauffeur's going as well," Thomas added.

"That's just brilliant," James said, throwing a piece of paper in the air. "Has he run off with the circus as well?"

"It's not the circus. Joseph is in a travelling variety show," Camilla said.

"And what about that girl, Lottie. I haven't seen her at all since we've been back."

At that moment Camilla shot me a look and I felt I should explain why Lottie was no longer in the employment of the hotel. I approached the desk but noticed that Hamilton did not follow.

"Mr Millar, may I give you my sincere apologies," I said as I reached the counter.

"For what?" he asked.

"My lady," Camilla said under her breath to her husband, reminding him of the etiquette.

"My lady," Mr Millar said between his teeth. "What is it you feel obliged to apologise for?"

"The maid, Lottie, is now employed by myself as my assistant. I booked an extended stay here for three months and I hired her after she showed an affiliation with my dog, who she keeps under control."

He frowned. "The young woman who was with you just now?"

"We'll be losing even more customers to The Grand Hotel," Thomas said. "With all the staff leaving."

"I don't need the reminder," James Millar said but thankfully the volume of his voice had been adjusted. "We can't function with a handful of staff."

I heard the footsteps of someone approaching from behind and turned to see Mr Breckon hurrying from his office towards us.

"It's true that The Grand is in a better location for the nightlife," Camilla said with a sigh. "But we're popular due to our reputation."

"Our reputation was dashed in our absence." James Millar gave Breckon a stare full of accusation as he reached him. "I wish we'd never taken that trip to India." He looked back at Thomas. "For many reasons."

"Is there a problem?" Breckon asked, clearly struggling to remove the weary sigh from his voice. "I was on the telephone to the butcher. I've negotiated a ten percent discount."

Camilla sighed. "We'll probably need more than that."

"I'm sure things will pick up," I said in a cheery

voice. "It's such a beautiful hotel and summer is not yet in full swing." As I stood there, I convinced myself that I was needed in amongst the fray to diffuse the situation and that it had nothing to do with my nosiness.

"We took a lot of trade from The Grand when we opened," Camilla said to me. "I used to work there. Angus Scott taught me everything I know."

"In more ways than one," James added with a grumble.

"James." She gave him a warning glare then turned back to me. "My husband spent so much time there as a guest before he received his inheritance. We were all rather close friends." She sighed. "Maybe this is our payback."

"It'll be that insufferable man spreading the lies about food poisoning," Mr Millar said. "He said he would get his revenge. And this is it." He shook his head.

"Father often refers to business as dog eat dog," Thomas said.

"A man who has no sense of economics," James Millar said. "Like father, like son."

Camilla gave a nervous look, as she glanced between her husband and her nephew. "Why don't we all calm down," she said before turning to me. "When we first opened, the fashionable set were prepared to walk up the hill and pay extra to be in our surroundings with the exceptional view."

"I heard this spot used to be a children's home

before the war," I said remembering Mr Breckon telling me this when I had arrived.

Camilla put a hand to her chest. "It was and James spent a few years here after his parents died."

"Oh my goodness," I said looking at her husband.

James gave his wife a hard stare, clearly not pleased that she was detailing his history. Still, it was extremely interesting.

Camilla placed a hand on James's arm. "His aunt could not take him in at the time but when her husband passed away, James moved in with her and lived in Bristol."

"I think that's enough family history for one day," James grumbled.

"I'm sorry, but I'm very proud of you and what we've achieved here." Camilla turned back to me. "We took down the existing building as it had become unsafe and rebuilt this modern style building, appointing one of the best architects in England. As popular as we've been, we've yet to pay off our original investment."

"Our? You mean my original investment," James grumbled as he flipped through a pile of invoices.

"It's a beautiful building," I said.

"It should be for the amount it cost. Not forgetting the switchboard *she* had me install so we could have phones in every room." He shook his head. "You'd think it was The Savoy."

"We said we were a modern hotel. It's what people come for." Camilla turned to me. "With our evening shows and dances, we soon became the number one choice. The Grand Hotel used to provide traditional music and entertainment. But now Angus Scott has updated the shows at The Grand, which is on the doorstep to many of the jazz bars which have opened up in recent months." She sighed. "It's our hotel that brought the Bright Young Things to Branden Bay in the first place. It seems wrong that we've now been abandoned."

The telephone rang.

"Millar's Hotel," James Millar said as he answered. He turned away and lowered his voice. "It's not a convenient time."

"Is there something I can help you with, my lady?" Mr Breckon asked as he stepped behind the counter. His eyebrows were raised, clearly noticing that I was listening in to Mr Millar's telephone conversation.

I smiled at him. "I wanted to check to see if I had any messages," I lied, whilst at the same time continuing to listen to the owner's call.

"We'll talk when I see you. Three o'clock." James put the phone down, looking more than a little flustered.

"Who was that?" Camilla asked, tight-lipped.

"I've business to attend to," James said, tidying the pile of invoices and placing them back in the drawer.

"It better had be business," Camilla said with a huff.

"I'll check on the kitchen to see what menu the cook suggests for today," Thomas said, clearly wanting to get away from his warring uncle and aunt.

"It'll probably only be us that eats it," Camilla called

after him with a sigh. "Most guests are eating in town to avoid being poisoned."

"We'll be dining in for an early meal this evening," I said. "We have a sightseeing trip booked for this afternoon. The Earl of Garthorn will be joining us. If you could alert me when he arrives?" It was a grand title for a young man of eighteen. And if he did as his family wished he would one day become the Marquis of Bandberry. "Lord Garthorn's train home is at seven."

"Of course, my lady," Camilla said.

"We're happy with home-cooked food. The young man was saying to me when we met that he prefers simple cuisine. So please let Mrs Lloyd know one that of her pies accompanied by seasonal vegetables will suffice."

Camilla gave a smile of relief. "I will do. And I hope you have a lovely day, my lady."

"Not another cancellation?" Mr Millar grumbled as he turned to the next page of the bookings diary.

Prince barked and I turned my head to see that Lottie was back from the garden. I left the reception desk to join them. She was talking in a hushed voice to Hamilton at the foot of the stairs. Probably about me and my inquisitive nature since they stopped speaking when I reached them.

"I'll fetch us a pot of tea for the suite," Lottie said, handing me Prince's leash.

Under usual circumstances, I would have insisted a member of the hotel staff bring the tea to my room, but as the hotel employees were so thin on the ground, I let her go.

We took a steady walk up the stairs with Prince at my heels. I heard the tap of Hamilton's walking stick on the stairs behind me. He was not at all lame but had suffered severe shell shock from the war and continued to carry his stick as a mental crutch. He had told me he intended to do so until such a time that he felt cured. It saddened me that he still had it with him. I remembered well the nightmares he had been plagued with whilst he was convalescing at Ashcombe Hall and I shuddered at the thought that they must still be a part of his life.

As we reached the top floor, Lottie came out of the service lift. "Norma said she will bring the tea up to us. I think she wants to see you."

"That's nice," I said.

"I think she rather wants to gossip with you, Lady Ellen," Hamilton said. "Maybe I will sit out of your way on the balcony with Prince."

I smiled, guessing that Hamilton was correct in his assumption as we entered the suite. I was pleased to have a suite and to be able to entertain guests in a respectable manner. Prince followed Hamilton as he walked through the living area then through the French doors to the balcony. Whilst he had enjoyed our investigation, I knew he was not comfortable with gossip for gossip's sake.

CHAPTER 3

$\mathcal{T}$here was a knock at the door of my suite and I answered it to find a red-faced Norma Lloyd staring at me.

"My lady." Her hands gripped a trolley upon which was placed a large tea pot, an array of biscuits and a Victoria sponge. "I've brought cake, although it's yesterday's. But I just had to talk to someone. I always feel so much better chatting to you, my lady. And you did say I could talk to you any time."

I smiled at her. "Indeed. I've told you on many occasions, Mrs Lloyd, that I'm happy to lend an ear, should you have any problems."

Lottie took a cup of tea and balanced two biscuits on the saucer then delivered it to Hamilton on the balcony. I looked through the window panes and saw him reading the newspaper with Prince at his feet. It warmed my heart to see the pair together.

Once I had settled on the settee with Lottie, I

encouraged Norma Lloyd, who was sitting in the armchair opposite us, to begin.

"I understand the chef has left?" I said.

"The whole place is falling apart, my lady. One minute we're the talk of the town, the next no one wants to come here. And I don't blame them neither." She sighed. "I'll be losing my job next."

"They won't want you to leave," Lottie said. "Even if it means you're only providing meals for the Millars."

"And that nephew of his. Well, I don't mean to speak ill of my employer's family but he's as useless as feathers on a fish. Born with a silver spoon in his mouth. He knows nothing and when me and John did manage to get a night off, we saw him down Jake's Jazz Club, drinking and blabbing his mouth off about the state of his uncle and aunt's marriage. The lad has no shame." She shook her head. "After the hospitality they've shown him."

I leaned forward. "He seemed pleasant enough."

"It's a front. He was telling the barman that he only came here because he heard the hotel was a money trap and he wanted a free ticket to England." She shook her head. "Poor Mr and Mrs Millar I know just how they feel." She picked up a napkin and dabbed her eye.

"About what?" Lottie asked.

"Oh, it's just me being silly. The late Mr Lloyd and me, we couldn't have children neither. And Mr Millar has brought that waste of space back here as a replacement son and young Thomas's taking it all for granted. He was treated like a king in Calcutta. He didn't even have to open a door. Wouldn't surprise me if he never even wiped his own…"

"Mrs Lloyd," Hamilton called from the balcony. "Lovely biscuits."

"Er, thank you, Captain," Mrs Lloyd said as she blushed. She lowered her voice. "My John says Thomas is nothing but a lounge lizard." Norma was having a romance with John Breckon, the manager of the hotel. She drained her tea. "I don't know what to do about it. Should I tell Mr Millar what Thomas says behind his back?"

Lottie refilled Norma's cup and handed it to her. "He might think you're making it up."

"Exactly," Norma said, leaning back in the chair and holding her cup with both hands. "I don't want to ask for trouble." She took a thoughtful sip of her hot drink.

"You're extremely talented, Mrs Lloyd," I said. "If you decided to speak your mind and found yourself without work, you could easily find another position." I wondered whether I could find her work in Ashcombe. I did so like her pies.

Norma shook her head. "I'm not leaving my John." Her relationship with the manager was only in its early months.

"Very admirable of you," I said. "Now let's enjoy your wonderful sponge."

"What have you planned for today, my lady?" she asked me.

"After luncheon, we're going to the castle for a tour."

"Mary's showing us around," Lottie said eagerly and then bit into her cake.

Norma reached for a slice and huffed. "If it wasn't for her, the hotel might still be on its feet."

"Why do you say that?" I asked.

"If she hadn't had a thing for Mr Millar they wouldn't have gone away to repair their marriage in India. If they were here when Major Coltrane died, and were able to support the hotel, we might have come out unscathed. That Mary has a lot to answer for."

"Mrs Millar wasn't perfect either, was she?" Lottie said. "Everyone knows she had something going on with Angus Scott at The Grand and he's married as well."

Norma tutted. "His wife, there's another lost soul. She's a recluse. I heard she lost all her hair then it grew back white." She shook her head. "That's what stress can do to you."

"What sort of stress?" I asked.

"She always suffered with her nerves. She had a difficult childhood. One of the misplaced children that made a life in Branden Bay after leaving the children's home."

"Like James Millar?" I asked, remembering that Camilla had told us he had lived at the home.

"He only spent three years in the place. Dora was there for her entire childhood. She used to work at The Grand and that's how she met Angus Scott. Did well for herself, probably because she was such a beauty." She glanced at the clock on the mantelpiece. "Oh, bless me, look at the time. I'd better get the meat on for the pie and make sure the bread has come in for your sandwiches." She smiled at me. "Thanks for listening to me, my lady. I know I go on a bit." She stood up. "I feel much better."

"And you make me feel quite at home," I said. "As I have told you before, back at Ashcombe Hall I spend at least a half hour chatting with my kitchen staff." I thought back to my employees and had to admit I was rather missing them.

WE LATER ENJOYED a sandwich luncheon in the hotel's beautiful orangery. The glass annex was tagged onto the building and housed exotic plants which contrasted with the well-established shrubs and bushes in the gardens outside. I guessed those had been there from when the site was a children's home. After chatting about the changes in the town since I had visited it as a child, it was time to meet Sebastian. As we left the orangery, the young man had just arrived from the railway station. He raced up to Lottie, held both of her hands and looked down at her as she gazed back up at him.

"You look even more beautiful with that new hair-do," he said, admiring her new bobbed haircut.

Lottie beamed at him. "Thank you. Ellen took me to the barber. I was so nervous," she giggled.

"It looks super," he said.

She put the hat on which I had given her. I had

passed on a couple of the dresses I had commissioned for the trip, too. It gave me so much joy to see how happy and appreciative she was.

Camilla raised her eyebrows from the reception desk as we passed. She was probably well aware of the scandal Lottie had caused when in London. A romantic association between her and the young earl would no doubt be gossiped about amongst the hotel staff.

Once outside, Hamilton and I allowed Lottie and Sebastian to walk ahead of us as we took the aptly named Castle Road, which snaked through residential streets on its way to the town's well-known landmark.

"I love this town," Sebastian said. His voice was projected back to us by the wind as he marched ahead. Lottie stopped to catch her breath. It was a rather steep incline and became steeper the closer we got to our destination with the castle commanding a lofty position above the town. Sebastian stopped to allow Lottie to catch up and when she reached him, he reached out and took her hand. With her steps being much smaller than his, she was practically jogging beside him as they continued up the hill, with her other hand on top of her head to keep her hat on as the breeze picked up. I walked at a slower pace with Hamilton and held Prince's leash as he stopped to sniff every now and again at an array of interesting bushes, probably hoping to find a rabbit. As I regarded Lottie, I could see she was deeply in love. As charming as Sebastian was, he was somewhat naïve to think he could shun his family's wishes. Whilst I smiled at

Lottie's excitement, I could not help but anticipate a deeply broken heart.

"Mama forbids me to walk in London," Sebastian said, his voice being carried on the wind. "I must take the car everywhere." He stopped and dropped Lottie's hand, turning to face the slope we had just walked up. "I feel on top of the world." He outstretched his arms taking deep breaths. He turned back and hugged Lottie. For all my reservations about the relationship between the pair, I could see how much he adored her, even if his public display of affection was a little too modern. Especially for Hamilton, whose eyebrows shot up at the sight of the embrace. Hamilton had a keen sense of right and wrong and whilst he had not said as much, his disapproval and protective instinct were visible on his face. He was clearly concerned that Lottie was being taken advantage of.

We too turned around and admired the view of the bay. In the distance, people were dotted on the beach enjoying the sunshine. The water glistened underneath the rays. The fairground constantly moved with the rotating Ferris wheel and the cars snaking over the roller-coaster. Every now and again the wind brought snippets of music and squeals from those on the rides.

"The tide must have turned," Hamilton said. "The wind picks up when it's on its way in."

As we continued to admire the view, a large fellow trudged up the road with his head down. As he passed us his hat flew off, revealing a shock of red hair.

Sebastian retrieved the man's trilby from a bush

and brushed a leaf from it. "There you are, sir," he said as he handed it to him.

The gentleman nodded his thanks, replaced his hat and went on his way.

"Here," Hamilton said to me. "Let me take Prince."

"Thank you," I said, glad because I needed to hold onto my hat.

"It's so blustery," I called out to the others as the red-haired man marched up the hill ahead of us, but they did not hear me as a gust had whipped my words away. It was hard going but I felt free and it was exhilarating to spend time with these people – all of us from a different a social standing. Sebastian an earl, myself with land but only a courtesy title – my father had no male heir so the title of 'Earl of Ashcombe' had died with him. Then there was Hamilton, educated and middle class, and Lottie some way down from all of us. A girl brought up in service without a proper education, having been taught to read and write by the son of her employer, a young man who was now clearly in love with her. Lottie was so full of life and excitement, believing the world was her oyster and that the future Marquis of Bandberry would one day be her husband. And as I walked up the hill feeling completely alive, I suddenly believed it was possible too. That anything was possible.

I swayed and Hamilton held out his free hand for me and I grabbed it. I felt a warmth cover my body that told me I also wanted to cross the social lines for romance. I blushed and pushed the thought away.

When we reached Branden Bay Castle, it towered above us. Built of stone from the local quarry, it had two turrets to the front. With no moat, there were steps leading up to a large wooden door. A young woman stood at the foot of the steps smiling at us as we approached. She had a warm and welcoming expression and bright blue eyes with exceptionally dark brown hair.

"I'm pleased to meet you, Lady Ellen, Lord Garthorn and you too Captain Hamilton."

Lottie grinned at Mary. "Thanks for agreeing to the tour. I can't wait."

"Follow me," she said. "It's so windy out here, we'll go straight inside."

As we walked up the steps I turned to Mary. "Have you always had an interest in history?"

She nodded. "Yes, it's fascinating and although I loved working at Millar's Hotel, this is my dream job. Even if it's voluntary and I have to work in The Branden Arms by night to pay for my lodgings."

"It's admirable that you follow your passion," Sebastian said. "That is what I intend to do. And please call me Sebastian, I drop the title when away from home, it's so tiresome." He put his arm around Lottie's shoulders and she looked up at him with such adoration it nearly broke my heart.

Mary gave them a sweet smile with her head to one side. It was clear to everyone how much in love Lottie and Sebastian were.

As we went through the large door, a chill filled the

air with the type of dank smell I had experienced when on a cave tour in the village of Cheddar.

Lottie visibly shuddered. "It's a bit creepy. Polly from the kitchens said she saw a ghost here."

"Some say it's haunted," Mary said as the wind whistled through the windows.

Lottie stopped in her tracks.

I laughed. "There's no such thing as ghosts, Lottie."

"I'm sure there are," she said with a whisper, her eyes wide open. "Polly saw a woman in a white nightgown."

"I'm sure she was teasing you, Lottie," Hamilton said with a chuckle.

"It's thought the castle was constructed around 1524," Mary said.

"Wow, so it's four hundred years old," Lottie said, looking around the large room in which we stood. It was dominated by the huge fireplace.

"It was built by Sir William of Cleve as a symbol of prestige. Through the centuries it has been modernised by those who have lived here, including the creation of the ballroom. The castle has a history of being used as an entertainment venue." She led us to a large central space around which was a raised walkway. Many doors led off from this. Around the room were portraits. I knew the area was used for balls as I had attended one myself with Papa.

Mary gestured around the space. "These portraits show members of the family of years gone by."

"Amazing," Sebastian said. "I love reading family history."

"Through the turbulent years of the Civil War, the castle became a refuge for escaping nobility and during the English Reformation, they hid catholic priests."

"That's jolly interesting," Hamilton said.

"Who owns the castle now?" I asked.

"The Cleve family still own it, but no longer live here," Mary replied. "They live on the continent. The castle is managed by a charitable trust which maintains its historical value." Her explanation was clear. I was impressed with how Mary had memorised so much information about the castle.

We walked further through the castle listening to Mary's excellent knowledge. There were quite a few other visitors milling around. Some stopped and listened in as Mary imparted interesting facts.

Mary approached a set of armour. It was close to a large window and the sun streamed in, glinting on the metal. A man with a smooth and entirely bald head stood admiring it. He turned around stroking his beard as we approached, squinting through his spectacles as if trying to focus in, and then gave a smile as we neared.

"An interesting piece," he said in a broad Scottish accent. "I don't know about you," he said to Mary. "But I think it's older than the castle."

Prince snarled at the man, then growled.

I pulled at his leash to prevent any attack. "Prince, no!" I looked up to the man. "I'm so sorry. Prince is not fond of my game-keeper and he's Scottish as well. It's a warranted dislike, as the man tried to shoot him when he was a puppy." I stroked Prince's head to calm him.

The man chuckled. "I won't take it personally. I understand. And he's such a handsome dog."

Mary smiled at the man. "You're correct. William of Cleve was gifted this armour by his great-grandfather."

The Scottish man and Mary discussed the piece, including the detailed engravings, then we watched him limp away.

"If you could mind your heads," Mary said. "I'll take you up the turret. Unfortunately, we're unable to go to the very top on a windy day, as sadly more than one person over the years has toppled over the edge. But there's a window on the penultimate floor where you can enjoy an excellent view over the bay."

We took the spiral stone stairs and once on the penultimate floor we found the last stretch of stairs was roped off. The wind whooshed down the steps from above and I was glad that I'd decided to wear a coat. We took it in turns to look though the thin slits of the turret's windows.

"Millar's hotel looks stunning from here," I said gazing at the view of the white building.

"It's such a beautiful modern construction," Mary said. "I often said to James…Millar, how it looks like an angel with its wings spread out. The guardian of the bay I called it."

"I hear Mrs Millar designed the hotel," Hamilton said. I wondered whether he was ignorant of the fact that Mary had supposedly had an affair with James Millar or whether he was pressing the point home that James Millar was a married man.

"I understand the architect Emerson Price designed it." Mary gestured up the stairs. "James loves the view from up here."

Hamilton raised his eyebrows. Mary talking so candidly about a married man clearly did not gain his approval, no matter how bad the marriage was with Camilla.

"It's a shame that some people have cancelled their bookings at the hotel," Lottie said.

"I'm sure business will pick up once Coltrane's death is forgotten," Hamilton said. "One big event and it'll be back on the map."

"I hear we're in for a hot summer," Sebastian added as he stepped forward to take his turn to look through the window. "It's truly an amazing view. And yes, the hotel does resemble an angel. I'm sure the rest of the summer will bring people in their droves."

After we had all taken in the view, we took a slow and steady walk down the turret then headed for the second turret.

Mary pointed to the stone spiral steps. "Some say the left-hand turret is haunted by the ghost of Lady Astrid of Cleve who killed herself after her lover had been murdered."

"That's the ghost Polly saw," Lottie said. "She ran down the turret, right before her eyes."

Prince gave out a long and haunting wine which

echoed around the place giving an even eerier atmosphere. His canine wail clashed with the sound of the wind squealing through the thin windows.

"Can we go now?" Lottie asked in a small voice.

"Of course," Mary said. "And this is the end of my tour. Feel free to explore the rest of the castle. Maybe have a walk along the tunnels and take in the grounds. The gardens are truly magnificent and include an array of plant species and topiary." She gestured to her right. "I'll be in the ballroom gallery should you wish to find me with any further questions."

"Thank you, Mary. It's been most interesting and entertaining," Sebastian said to her.

"And you've gone half an hour over our allotted time," I added.

"Don't worry about that," Mary said. "I've really enjoyed myself and it's been lovely to see Lottie again." She gave a small sad smile. "I really miss being at the hotel."

"I found it fascinating," Hamilton said. "Really informative and you clearly know your subject. You could become a history teacher." I saw him take out some money and pass it discreetly to Mary.

She nodded at him with a blush. "Thank you. I'd love to become a teacher."

"Me too," Sebastian said. "I live for books and literature. I'll be reading English at Oxford."

"Sebastian is great at giving lessons. He taught me so much," Lottie said, looking up at him with a proud smile.

"Have fun exploring," Mary said. "Be careful if you take the tunnels and make sure you exit by half past five. I'm sure you won't want to be locked in all night."

"Maybe we should go outside now?" Lottie said, pulling on Sebastian's arm.

We all laughed and Prince barked.

Sebastian took her hand. "Come along. Let's have an adventure along the tunnels." He led her away as she protested.

I hesitated and glanced at Hamilton. "We should really not leave that pair alone, considering I'm supposed to be chaperoning."

"He seems like an admirable young man," Hamilton said. "But you have a point."

"Meet us at the front door in half an hour," I called out to them. As much as I felt obliged to do the decent thing, I had no wish to explore the tunnels myself.

After their laughter became distant, Hamilton smiled at me. "Let's take a closer look at the artwork." Hamilton pointed to his right. "I believe the portraits are this way."

"I hope Lottie and Sebastian will be safe in the tunnels," I said.

"Mary said they lead to the woods. I'd love to take a stroll amongst the trees one day."

"I'm sure we can arrange that. Maybe after our trip to Bristol?" I smiled at him. "I rather like being a tourist at last. I've not holidayed since before the war. Papa used to take me to many places, he spoiled me rotten after Mama died. Being a busy man, he made the times we spent together most exciting."

"You deserve time to breathe out, Ellen, after the work you did when Ashcombe Hall was a convalescent home." He paused. "Forgive me, I mean, Lady Ellen."

I laughed. "When no-one is in earshot, Ernest, I'm sure we can use less formality. I'm sure you've noticed that I have asked Lottie to call me Ellen."

A silence hung between us. It had been many years since we had spoken freely and called each other by our Christian names. When we first met, I had not told Hamilton that I was Lady Ellen of Ashcombe Hall. He had thought I was simply 'Nurse Ellen'.

We took a slow walk around the periphery of the central space, taking time to look at each portrait and read the words beneath, which told us the history of each person. Prince gave a single bark which echoed around the space and I felt a chill entering my bones.

"I feel like some air and think Prince may need a comfort break," I said.

On our way we passed the turret and Prince began to snarl.

"Do you think it really is haunted?" I asked Hamilton in a whisper.

As if on cue there was a long cry.

I jumped.

Hamilton laughed. "It's not a ghost. It's probably Sebastian fooling around."

Prince gave a long whine which echoed off the stone walls.

I shuddered, feeling the chill of the dank air. "Come along."

As we left through the large wooden door, the sun hit my eyes and I breathed in the fresh air. Grateful to be outside, I turned to the left, noticing a small crowd had formed. A man pointed to the floor beneath the turret. Another took his hat off and a woman descended into sobs.

Lottie and Sebastian came out behind us.

"What's going on?" Lottie asked.

"We heard someone cry out," Sebastian added with concern.

Mary appeared behind us. "I'll see what the commotion is about."

I watched her hurry over to the small gathering of people. The crowd parted for her as she reached them.

Mary let out a cry. "James." She slumped to her knees.

"Stay here," Hamilton said as he hurried over to investigate with his stick over his forearm. I felt cold as I watched him drop his stick to the floor and put his arm around Mary, asking a woman close by to assist. He pointed at a young fellow who then ran towards the exit.

"You don't think it's–?" Lottie stopped speaking as we heard Mary's sobs brought by the wind.

Hamilton left Mary in the care of the woman who had assisted him and returned to us, his expression was grave.

"Whatever has happened?" I asked as dread swished

around my stomach, already knowing what he was about to tell us.

Hamilton removed his hat and held it in his hands, his expression dark. "It appears that James Millar has fallen to his death."

CHAPTER 4

$\mathcal{T}$hree hours after James Millar had died, we were in the Seaview Restaurant. I sat at a table with Lottie, Hamilton, Sebastian and Prince. Beyond us the view from the window showed grey clouds marching towards us from the direction of Wales, as if mimicking the atmosphere in the room. Breckon sat on a table on his own with his head in his hands. Norma Lloyd hovered around Camilla as she wept, as if she did not know whether or not it would be appropriate to comfort her boss.

"He was only thirty-five," Camilla wailed. "I was meant to die before him. I can't imagine a day with him not being here."

"Let it all out," Norma said in a soothing voice which cracked, revealing her own emotion.

By the time we had returned to the hotel, the police had already delivered the devastating news to Camilla that her husband had fallen to his death. Sergeant

Chambers had left to meet the doctor who had been asked to inspect the body.

"The sergeant says they're asking the doctor to ascertain whether or not it was suicide," Camilla wailed. "Why would James do that?"

"Try and drink some brandy, Mrs Millar," Norma said to her. "It will help calm your nerves. I'm sure the doctor will be here as soon as he can, I asked him to visit to check on you."

The rest of the hotel had become even quieter with a constant trickle of guests leaving.

"But I've not got my hat and coat," a man said as he passed the restaurant doorway, carrying two sets of luggage.

"Leave them, let's get out of this place," his wife said. "It's cursed."

"Mr Breckon," Camilla said.

He looked up. "Yes?"

"Please get a message to all remaining guests that we're closing due to a family bereavement. I can't possibly cope at the moment."

He exchanged a worried glance with Norma. Clearly both were concerned for their future. He stood up and left the room.

"Where are we going to go?" Lottie whispered to me.

"Don't worry, wherever it is, I'm taking you with me," I reassured her. My trip to Branden Bay was certainly not turning out to be the relaxing holiday I'd planned.

"I want you to stay," Camilla said to us. "Please?"

"How kind," I said, not wanting to really commit. I had mixed emotions about remaining at Millar's. I'd felt an element of relief at the prospect of finding alternative accommodation. Possibly in another town, somewhere with a lot less drama. But Camilla was clearly distressed and I did not want to upset her further by rejecting her invitation.

"It was her I tell you, she was obsessed with him," Camilla said.

"Who?" Norma asked.

"That woman, Mary. He clearly went up to the castle to see her. It must have been her that called him this morning. I bet she pushed him off."

I exchanged a look with Lottie.

"I don't think Mary could have done that," Lottie said in a small voice.

"You don't know her," Camilla said. "There's a dark side to that woman. She got her claws into my James and wouldn't let go. He even said to me how much she begged him, how she flaunted herself and told lies about me, to turn him against me. She's got a touch of the Devil in her." She took deep breaths and attempted to speak in a clear tone. "When we were in India, James said he regretted every moment he'd spent with her. That there was only one woman…" She stopped as she burst into tears." She gasped. "He loved me, only me."

Prince whimpered and I stroked his head to calm him down as Camilla sobbed. I felt dreadful and my heart went out to her.

"Take slow, deep breaths," Norma said. "The police will get to the bottom of this, I'm sure."

"I'll reopen the hotel in time, it's everything to me," Camilla said with a hiccup. "I have to pull myself together." She wiped her eyes. "I'm going to make it work, to carry on and keep James's name alive. Millar's Hotel will rise again and be here for future generations to enjoy." She sniffed then looked at Norma. "You don't think the hotel is cursed, do you, like that man said?"

"No, of course not," Norma replied. "You aren't thinking straight."

Lottie shot me a look. She bit her lip. I shook my head at her. I didn't want her believing in curses as well as ghosts. Sebastian put his arm around her.

"The hotel has been wonderful for the town," I said. "You've had a great many people come here since you opened over a year ago."

"Yes, it's you and Mr Millar that brought people here," Norma said.

"It will be great again. I'm sure of it," Hamilton added in a gentle voice.

Camilla wiped her eyes. "When James's aunt left him such a large inheritance, James thought it was a gift from heaven." She gave another sob, then looked at me. "Little did he know, it was his death sentence. This would never have happened if he still lived in Bristol, doing his job as a clerk."

She dabbed her nose with her handkerchief. "I cannot accept that he jumped to his death. James would never have left me."

Thomas entered the room, his face ashen.

Breckon followed him in.

"I just heard what happened. Everyone in town is talking about it. I can't believe it." Thomas swayed a little and Breckon pulled a seat out for him. Thomas sat down. It was clear he had been drinking but had sobered to an extent, due to the shock. "Why would Uncle James do a thing like that? I knew he was upset with us this morning and angry with us losing business to The Grand, but to kill himself?" He stared at Camilla, blinking rapidly.

Breckon also took a seat at the same table. "It's terrible. Just terrible." He placed his head in his hands. I was worried about the manager's health. Two deaths in one month. And a once vibrant hotel was now a ghost ship. Recent events were clearly taking their toll on the man. I glanced out of the room and saw Polly, the kitchen maid, and David, the porter, walking through the reception area with their coats on, carrying cases. It appeared it was not only the guests who were leaving.

Camilla narrowed her eyes at Thomas. "He wasn't upset with me this morning." She gestured at him. "It was you he was disappointed with. I can assure you, before he left he…" The tears welled in her eyes again and she took a deep breath. "Your mother has a lot to answer for. If she hadn't been so insistent on James visiting her, we wouldn't have left the hotel and things would not have been in such a mess. James would not have had to deal with you!"

"Mrs Millar, maybe you need a lie down," Norma

said, her expression telling me she thought Camilla was about to lose her temper.

"Don't insult my mother," Thomas said, pointing at his aunt. "It's nothing to do with her. Uncle James told me the only reason you took such a long trip was because your marriage was in ruins. My family never forced you to visit." He lowered his head and spoke in a quieter tone. "Mother loved her younger brother. She'll be heartbroken when she hears about this." He shook his head. "And now I must send a telegram to my parents, to tell them this awful news." He stood up then took a deep breath.

Camilla also rose and pointed at him. "It's your mother's fault – If she missed her family, she shouldn't have moved so far away from England." Camilla gave Thomas a dismissive wave. "And now you're free to return to India. There's no need for you to stay here, now your uncle's gone. You never liked me, so let's not pretend we'll be working together. Go – pack your bags."

Breckon began coughing. I was worried the poor man would choke.

Norma flashed a worried look at him.

"I'm not going anywhere, other than to the post office to arrange the telegram," Thomas said. "The will hasn't been read yet."

Camilla gave a laugh. "You're not mentioned. And now we see your true colours."

"Young man," Hamilton said to Thomas. "I know you're upset about your uncle, but your aunt has just lost her husband. Her life partner – please calm things down. Words spoken in the heat of the moment can cause long-lasting harm."

"She's no longer my aunt, not now James has gone. There's no blood connection between us two."

"Show some respect," Hamilton demanded. "Mrs Millar has this hotel to contend with. I think you should offer your help and support." I knew that Hamilton hated it when men spoke dishonourably to women.

Thomas shook his head and pointed at his aunt. "You drove him to it, you're to blame. I've listened to you criticising Uncle James for endless hours, both in India and here and he told me he wanted a divorce."

"How dare you!" Camilla screamed, swaying, her eyes staring wildly at Thomas.

Norma steadied her boss.

"That is utter rubbish and you…" Camilla paused as if gasping for breath. "You're a thief. I know you stole the necklace from James. And so did he. He was about to throw you out!"

"It's you he wanted rid of, you're a liar. Everyone knows you've been with Angus Scott at The Grand. James knew you were about to deceive him. You were spotted there on Monday."

Hamilton stood up at this point and approached Thomas. "You need some air." Hamilton led Thomas out of the room in such a fashion he nearly lifted him off the floor.

"Let go of me," Thomas said shrugging Hamilton

off. "As I said, I'm off to the post office." He left the room but Hamilton followed him.

"He's just upset, Camilla," I said in what I hoped was a soothing voice.

"My whole world has fallen apart." Her voice changed to a whisper as she sat down. "How could Thomas say those hateful things at a time like this?" She burst into tears.

"Once he's calmed down, I'm sure Thomas will apologise," Norma said.

"Emotions run high in these situations," I said. "People say things they don't mean." I thought back with sadness to the day I was brought the news that my beloved husband, Leonard, had been taken from me. I could imagine how Camilla felt.

"I don't believe James would kill himself." She looked at me through tear-laden eyelashes. "Do you think he was pushed?" she asked in a whisper.

I took a deep breath and considered my next words. I had been convinced that my late husband Leonard had been murdered when everyone else told me it was an accident. I needed to distance myself from that situation and not taint my judgement or encourage Camilla to think likewise. But at the same time, the thought of one's husband committing suicide was another bitter pill to swallow. "Maybe he tripped and fell?" I said.

"The wind was ferocious," Sebastian added. "It could have been an unfortunate accident. The top of the turret was out of bounds."

Camilla stood up. "I intend to find out exactly what happened. I'm calling Scotland Yard."

Oh no, I thought, not relishing the possibility of a reappearance of Inspector Stone. We'd not seen eye to eye on his last investigation. To say that Inspector Stone was not fond of me was an understatement.

"Come on, Mrs Millar," Norma said. "I'll take you to your room and we can wait for Dr Field." She approached Camilla. At this point, tears were also falling down Norma's cheeks. It was a very sad day for the hotel.

Once they were out of the room, I let out a long slow breath and glanced at Lottie. "Do you and Sebastian want to take Prince out?" I said.

Sebastian appeared relieved to be asked as he stood up with my dog's leash in his hand.

"Are you all right, Ellen?" Lottie asked. I presumed my expression was weary.

"Yes, of course. You go along with Sebastian and Prince."

I was left alone with Breckon, who remained with his head in his hands. I felt the need to calm the poor man down.

"Don't worry, Mr Breckon. Once Mrs Millar has got over the shock, I'm sure she'll be able to pull the business back to its former glory. Speaking from experience, life does go on. You both have a wealth of knowledge and I'm sure you'll be able to turn it around."

Breckon shook his head. "That won't happen. This is bad, really bad."

"I know. It's always a shock when someone so young dies. My husband was even younger than James Millar – he was still in his twenties."

Breckon stared at me with his lips parted as if he was about to say something then shut his mouth.

"Is there something else troubling you?" I asked gently. Clearly there was as he was not calming down at all.

"I'm afraid I feel unable to speak of it, my lady."

My curiosity got the better of me at this stage and I moved from my table to join him. Pulling a chair out I sat opposite. "I'm discreet, Mr Breckon." He looked burdened and I convinced myself I was caring for his health. "A problem shared is a problem halved."

He looked around as if checking we were still alone. "Mr Millar changed his will," he whispered then covered his mouth as if the fact had escaped it without his permission.

"Changed?" I asked.

"Very recently, only a matter of days ago."

"And how do you know this?" I leaned further towards him.

Breckon took his handkerchief from his pocket and mopped his brow. "I witnessed it." He shook his head. "She'll be furious."

"So I take it this change will upset Mrs Millar?" I asked, nearly gulping myself.

He slowly nodded his head. "Mr Millar left–"

He was interrupted by the telephone ringing on the reception desk, which sounded louder in the now sparsely occupied hotel. "I must answer that but do not breathe a word to anyone." He stood up and hurried away.

I now felt burdened by what he'd told me, yet I had no clue as to the contents of the will. All I knew was that Camilla would not be happy. But whatever James Millar's wishes were, the details would come out soon enough. I realised that unless I made an alternative booking, we would again be in the middle of a full-scale drama. As inquisitive as I was, this was not what I wanted for my planned break by the sea. I sighed as I stood up. Hearing a bark, I looked towards the doorway to find that Lottie and Sebastian had returned with Prince.

"We think he wants a long walk, Ellen," she said.

"So do I," I replied and stood up. "I'd love to go to the beach and you'll require a chaperone. We must not forget that."

Lottie gave Sebastian a sideways glance as if I had scuppered their plans.

Mr Breckon rushed in. "It was the solicitor that telephoned. He heard about the death. He said he was coming here for a reading today, but I told him Mrs Millar is too distressed. He said he'll be here tomorrow afternoon in this restaurant at two p.m. he'll be asking all the beneficiaries to attend." He took his handkerchief out again. "Camilla will be in a rage when she sees it."

"Let's not get ahead of ourselves." I wanted to ask him outright for the details of the will but with Lottie and Sebastian in the room, Breckon was unlikely to divulge them. "As the guests are being asked to leave, maybe you would like to take Mrs Lloyd out this evening? To enable you to wind down. I can keep an eye on Mrs Millar." I had no idea why I suggested that – I would have enjoyed time to myself but the poor man surely needed the break for health reasons.

Hamilton returned to the room also.

"Ellen," Lottie said. "There's something else you should know. Sebastian has missed his train."

I raised my eyebrows. "I think there are more than enough rooms available here but I'm not sure it's decent." I pursed my lips, not disguising my disapproval.

"Sebastian can bunk in with me," Hamilton said. "If there's any question of impropriety, I can vouch for him."

"Thank you, Captain," Sebastian said.

We were interrupted by a shrill voice echoing from the reception.

"What on earth has happened here? Where is everyone?"

I looked up to find Mrs Flint, the housekeeping manager, standing in the doorway of the Seaview Restaurant with a small suitcase in her hand.

Breckon looked at her as if he was going to weep. "Ina, I'm afraid that you may wish to take a seat."

"Tell me what the matter is," she demanded.

Breckon took a deep breath. "James Millar has died having suffered a fall up at the castle." His voice wavered as he delivered the bad news.

"Oh, my dear Lord." Mrs Flint walked into the room, placed her case on the floor and steadied herself by holding onto the back of a chair. "How's Camilla?"

"Not good. Norma's with her in her room," Breckon said. "Thomas Jenkins is also here, James's nephew."

"He's gone into town to send an emergency telegram to his family," Hamilton added. "I warned him that the postmaster may not open up for him and that he might have to wait until the morning."

"If not, I'm sure he will end up in a bar," Breckon said with a shake of his head.

"I needed to distance him from Mrs Millar," Hamilton said. "I put him in a taxicab."

"We've now asked all guests to leave – the hotel is officially closed," Breckon added.

"I'll go up and see Mrs Millar," Mrs Flint said having composed herself already. Her brusque manner was exactly what was needed. It also meant that I was not required to sit with Camilla that evening.

CHAPTER 5

The following morning, I took Prince for a long walk, alone. Rather than taking him immediately to the beach, I took Castle Road. I could not eradicate Mr Millar's death from my mind. Was he driven to jump off the turret? As the castle came into view a Union Flag was flying at half-mast. As I slowly approached the castle grounds, I saw a sign to say they were closed for the day out of respect but would reopen as usual for the rest of the week. I stood still for a moment before taking a slow walk down to the town.

In Branden Bay High Street, life was going on as usual. The shops were opening whilst visitors and residents alike took breakfast. For most of the world it was just another day. Prince tugged me towards the seafront and I took in the details for memory's sake as I planned to leave at the earliest opportunity. With the bad luck that had befallen me since coming to this

56

beautiful town, I decided it would be prudent to return to Ashcombe Hall a lot sooner than planned.

After a long walk along the beach, I arrived at the hotel to find the last remaining guests filtering out. The doors were not locked but a large notice had been placed on the window, advising that Millar's Hotel was closed for the foreseeable future due to a family bereavement.

I took Prince through to the kitchen to ask for a bowl of fresh water and found Lottie, Hamilton and Sebastian taking breakfast around the large oak table. We were the only remaining guests and with no staff, we had been asked to help ourselves. Norma Lloyd and Breckon were also there.

"I'm so sorry, my lady, my lord," Norma said, nodding towards both Sebastian and me. "This is not an appropriate place for people of your standing. I'm sure you won't be charged for your rooms."

"We're here to support you, Mrs Lloyd," I said. "And we're more than happy to eat here with you. We would not expect to be served at a time like this."

"I'm jolly happy not to be waited on," Sebastian added. The young man seemed to relish the situation we had found ourselves in.

"It's a terrible business," Breckon said, shaking his head.

I made no comment, I had no idea whether Breckon had told anyone else that Camilla would not like the contents of the will. I had neither mentioned it to Hamilton nor Lottie. The will was to be read in a matter of hours, so everyone would know soon enough. I was rather pleased that I would not be present to witness Camilla's reaction.

Lottie handed me a slice of bread which she had cut and I spread a thin covering of butter onto it, followed by some strawberry conserve. "I think it may do you some good to get out of the hotel, Mr Breckon." I nodded at Norma. "You could both go for a pleasant walk, there's a breeze but the sun's shining."

"Lady Ellen's right, John. Let's do that."

"And how's young Thomas?" Hamilton asked. "Has he calmed down?"

"We found him in The Branden Arms," Breckon said.

"We couldn't face any of the music clubs, all that raucous atmosphere when poor James is dead," Norma said. "It didn't seem right."

Breckon turned to Norma. "Although The Branden Arms is no place for a lady."

"I didn't want to leave John on his own last night… not while he's worrying." She stopped as if she didn't mean to say that and I guessed Breckon had already confided in her about the contents of the will. "Although when we left," Norma continued, "Thomas was speaking to that Crow character." Norma shook her head. "He'll get himself into trouble if he carries on like that."

"I'll warn him today," Breckon said. "Simon Crow can be charming when he chooses to be. And then when he's got your attention, he dishes out a threat that would make any man's blood turn cold."

As I watched Breckon, I got the impression he'd been on the receiving end of Crow's harassment himself. We'd come across Simon Crow when investigating events leading to Major Coltrane's death. He was a fearsome looking fellow who had grown up in the area, with a dark beard and an always present flat cap. He'd been involved but I assumed the police let his part in the matter go. The local sergeant had told me at the time that Simon Crow had been evading the police for years. His words repeated in my head. *He's a real slippery character.*

Breckon shook his head. "Crow will take advantage of Thomas. He runs this town and with James gone, there's no one to advise the young man. He's lived a sheltered life. I doubt he'll listen to me."

"Mrs Millar will hopefully take him under her wing if he decides to stay," I said. "I'm sure they'll make up and work together once emotions settle down."

Breckon and Norma exchanged a glance and there followed a silence which Hamilton broke.

"Did he return in one piece?" Hamilton asked.

"We were in here having a cocoa before bed," Norma said, "and he got back as we were leaving. Made an awful mess after making himself a sandwich, which I had to clean up this morning. I doubt he'll get up until much later."

Mrs Flint entered the kitchen. "Camilla's awake. I

said I'll fetch some tea. She's still refusing to eat anything."

Lottie stood up. "I'll make it," she said.

Mrs Flint sat at the table. "I received contact from the solicitor. He asked for myself and Thomas to attend the reading of the will."

I glanced at Breckon as he continued to stare into his cup.

"Camilla said she wants the staff there as support," Mrs Flint added.

Mr Breckon looked up, the colour draining from his face. "Are you sure it's not a private affair?"

"Camilla wants you there. She wants us to toast James afterwards with champagne." She gestured at Norma. "She'd like you to make ginger biscuits." Her voice wavered. "James's favourite."

"So much for our walk," Norma muttered under her breath.

I could tell that Mrs Flint was silently grieving her late boss.

"How long have you been working for the Millars?" I asked Mrs Flint.

"Since they opened but I've known James since he was a lad. I worked at the children's home which was here. It was my first job. He was different to the other kids, he'd had a privileged upbringing, but was orphaned. His sister was placed with their paternal grandmother but there was not enough room for him also. His aunt took him in after three years, when her husband passed away." She gestured around the room.

"Then of course, when she died she left him a fortune which he used to build this place."

"What happened to the children's home?" I asked.

"They closed it during the war and used it as a hospital. The place was so run down that James decided to demolish it and rebuild from scratch. It was Camilla who oversaw the design of it all, though. They made a good team." Her voice broke and she blinked rapidly, clearly not wanting to cry in front of us.

"It's a great tragedy," I said as I stood up, not wanting to embarrass Mrs Flint who was close to tears. "We'll get out of your way."

"She wants you there as well," Mrs Flint said, composing herself.

"Me?" I said, with a hand to my chest, already concocting an excuse in my mind.

"Absolutely. And Captain Hamilton and Lottie too."

"Of course we will," Hamilton said, unaware that there was an impending commotion.

"I think I need some air," I said. "Come along Lottie, let's walk Sebastian to the station." I turned to the young man. "You don't want to miss another train and run the risk of your parents being alerted to your absence from Gosford Hall."

We left the kitchen and walked through the empty reception. As we reached the front door, Sergeant Chambers was walking across the threshold. I had become acquainted with him during the investigation into the death of Major Coltrane. He was an amiable man, unlike his colleague from Scotland Yard.

"Mrs Millar is not yet fit to see anyone, I'm afraid," I said. "She's still in her rooms."

"The reading of the will is planned to take place at two o'clock today," Hamilton said. "You may wish to return to speak to her tomorrow?"

"It can't wait and I've also come to see you, my lady," he said. "And your acquaintances." He nodded towards Hamilton, Lottie and Sebastian.

"Us?" I asked.

"You were at the castle yesterday and it's customary for us to prepare a report on the matter." He avoided eye contact.

Feeling a burn in my chest, I got the impression that Chambers may have thought James's death was not an accident.

"Sergeant, do you suspect foul play?" Hamilton asked, clearing picking up the same signal.

"Was it murder?" Lottie asked with her eyes wide open.

"As you were at the scene," Chambers said, "I should be grateful if you would remain in town until I have heard from Scotland Yard as to how they wish to proceed. I may need to take statements from you."

"All four of us?" I asked, realising that would be an issue for Sebastian.

"Yes, until I know Scotland Yard's wishes."

I guessed Chambers had a significant reason to believe it was murder and I shuddered. *Poor James Millar,* I thought.

"Will Inspector Stone be involved?" I asked.

"I can't predict any of the details, my lady."

Breckon arrived in the reception. "Can I help you, Sergeant Chambers?"

"I need to speak to Mrs Millar."

As he insisted on speaking to Camilla, I guessed he was serious. Breckon led Chambers away.

Lottie's eyes widened at Sebastian. "Will you get into trouble if you stay any longer in Branden Bay? Are they getting back to the hall today?"

"Yes, they will return and if my parents get wind of it, I will be in a spot of bother. I shall telephone Gosford Hall and leave a message for my aunt and uncle informing them that I'm unwell. I will hopefully be permitted to return tomorrow as Aunt Rose is likely to report any lengthy absence to my parents. It took a great deal of persuasion for Mama to allow me to visit Bristol, with it being only twenty miles from this town. They, of course, know that Lottie is here." He smiled at her. "I will say I have a stomach ailment and that I'm too ill to travel."

"Where do your aunt and uncle think you are?" I asked. Having met them before, I knew they were far from a modern couple.

"In the City of Bath, with an old school chum."

I felt a flutter of nerves that there may be an upset on the horizon.

"I'm so sorry, it's all my fault," Lottie said. "You could get into a lot of trouble."

Sebastian smiled at her. "It's their doing for banishing you from my life."

"I booked the tour of the castle." She looked at me. "Maybe we should've taken the boat to Bristol and met Sebastian there."

"Lottie," Sebastian took her hands. "Even if my parents find out, I'll have to have the discussion with them at some point. My life plan is not the same as the one they have in mind for me."

I was convinced it was a discussion that would not go well.

"Shall we take a walk anyway?" Hamilton asked.

Prince barked.

"If there's been foul play, I suggest we get ahead of ourselves. Especially if the troublesome Inspector Stone will be returning to Branden Bay," I said.

"You mean you want to investigate?" Sebastian asked me eagerly.

Prince barked again and pulled at his leash.

I nodded. "Let's talk and walk. Prince is eager to get outside."

Once on the pavement, I turned to Lottie. "Do you know where Mary lives?"

She pointed ahead. "Along Castle Road."

"I think we should pay her a visit and find out what she told the police in her statement. Of course, I would also like to check on her well-being. Let's go via the High Street."

After buying a beautiful bouquet from the florist, we took Castle Road and arrived at Mary's home. It was a three-storey detached building described as

'Castle Mansions' and was split into six separate tenements.

"Mary's on the ground floor," Lottie said as she pressed the bell.

Mary's landlady answered. She was a grey-haired woman dressed in a drab black dress.

"Hello, Mrs Swain," Lottie said as she held the bouquet of flowers. "We're calling to see how Mary is."

"She's not well," Mrs Swain said with a weary sigh.

"Who is it?" Mary called out in a weak voice from the doorway to her lodgings.

"It's Lottie and some others," Mrs Swain said. "Come along inside and I'll make a pot of tea." She turned away and bustled off.

Mary appeared in the long dark passageway and motioned for us to follow her. "I've been in pieces since yesterday." She burst into tears again.

"I can stay outside with the dog," Sebastian said.

"Bring him in, Mrs Swain won't mind," Mary said, gesturing for him to follow us inside. "She had a dog herself up until recently."

Mrs Swain, who had overheard, returned. "Give the leash to me, I'll give him a treat in my kitchen. And I'll put those flowers in water."

Prince barked and I could tell he was going to have an awful lot of fuss made of him.

CHAPTER 6

$\mathcal{M}$rs Swain's front room was decorated in a traditional Victorian style which suited the high-ceilinged room. We took our places upon her suite consisting of two settees and an armchair, all covered in a green fabric which had faded in patches where the sun came in from the huge sash windows. I admired the fireplace which was unlit since it was summertime. It was dressed with clean logs arranged in the hearth. I imagined Mrs Swain sitting there reading a book from one of the huge floor to ceiling bookcases built into the recesses either side of the fireplace.

Mrs Swain came into the room. "I have let your dog into the garden. It's completely walled off." She placed the flowers now in a glass vase, on the sideboard.

"I'm sure he'll enjoy sniffing around," I said with a smile.

"I'm lucky being on the ground floor and having a garden space."

"What an impressive library of books you have," Sebastian said to Mrs Swain as he stood, admiring them.

"Feel free to have a look through," she said. "They belonged to my husband. I don't read much myself and not those. He liked to sit for hours in his own little world." She sighed. "I miss him so much. First he went, then me dog. I tell you, Mary here has been a blessing lodging with me." She gestured at her dishevelled tenant. "You love reading them don't you, my dear."

Mary nodded in silence as Sebastian picked a book out, raising his eyebrows. "I see your husband was fond of his history, Mrs Swain."

"He liked all sorts," she said with a sad smile. "I'll get back and bring the tea in." She left the room.

I looked around the rest of the room, Mrs Swain had clearly not followed fashion with her décor but I found the room comforting, reminding me of Ashcombe Hall when I was a child. Although of course, on a much smaller scale. For a moment no one spoke and all we could hear was Sebastian turning pages of the book as he leafed through it and the tick from the mantelpiece clock.

I turned to Mary. "I hope you're feeling better. It's always a shock when someone we're close to passes away. I've had my own fair share of grief."

"I still can't believe it," Mary said and took a juddering inward breath.

"What do you think happened?" I asked gently.

"I honestly don't know," she said.

"Do you think he…meant to do it?" Lottie asked in a quiet voice.

"Never. He wouldn't do that," Mary said. "It's what the police kept asking me earlier today. I told them yes, he may have toppled over the edge, that's why it's roped off. It was dangerous up there but James wouldn't have… He would not have done it on purpose, he had so much to live for. He had plans for the future. We used to talk for hours about how he wanted to build a spa and bring people from far and wide for the Turkish bath, steam rooms and sauna." She sniffed and wiped her nose. "The police kept asking me what enemies James had and who was up there that day."

"Was Mr Millar at the castle to meet you?" I asked, watching for a reaction.

Mary turned her head away, then back to me. "I'd met him briefly when passing him in the street and he said he couldn't talk out in the open. He said he would explain. I guess he must have come on the spur of the moment, then saw I was conducting a tour with you and was up there, waiting for me to finish."

"On the top of a turret which was marked as out of bounds?" Sebastian asked, replacing one book on the shelf and picking up another.

"I guess he didn't want to be spotted," Mary said.

"Unless he had made a prior arrangement to meet someone else there?" Hamilton gave me a sideways glance. We both knew James Millar had arranged to meet someone at three o'clock – and that was the time he'd died.

Mary sighed. "Who knows what was going through his mind. James didn't always follow the rules. He often pushed the boundaries."

"If he was meeting someone up there, he might have chosen the turret because he did not want to be disturbed," Lottie said.

Sebastian added. "A roped off area is ideal if you want to stay out of sight."

"Did you telephone him yesterday morning?" I asked, knowing that someone had called him at the hotel.

"No." Mary shook her head. "We don't have a telephone here and I was up at the castle all day and there's no telephone there either. Why do you ask?"

I looked at Hamilton and he nodded, agreeing with me that it would be fine to share the information. "James arranged to meet someone at three o'clock and we don't know who it was."

"Oh," Mary said with a frown then lowered her head. "So he wasn't there to see me at all?" She shook her head sadly.

Mrs Swain wheeled a hostess trolley into the room.

Mary sat up straight. "I guess I was just hoping he was there to see me." She took a deep breath. "I guess I'll never know."

"I reckon he was pushed," Mrs Swain said as she

began pouring out cups of tea and adding milk and sugar without asking us if we cared for it.

"Don't be so dramatic, Judy," Mary said taking the first cup. "He must have slipped. I doubt he was killed at the castle."

"Then why was Sergeant Chambers asking you all those questions?" Mrs Swain said.

Mary shrugged. "I don't know what to think."

"That man was trouble for you, in life and in death," Mrs Swain said shaking her head at Mary. "Everyone knowing you and he were–"

"Friends," Mary cut her off. "No matter what our feelings were…" She looked at me. "Sorry if I'm being inappropriate."

"Not at all, Mary," I said. "A man has died, feel free to express yourself as you wish."

"He still dragged you into all that mess with his wife and got tongues wagging." Mrs Swain handed me a cup and saucer decorated with pink roses.

"Thank you, what a pretty cup," I said, guessing this was her best tea service.

Mrs Swain gestured at Mary. "The way he took advantage of you, instead of working on his own relationship. If you ask me he deserved all he got. And I would have told the police that too, if he hadn't been killed. I don't want to be their number one suspect." She rubbed her neck as if imagining the hangman's noose around it. She continued to pour the teas and Mary gave her a disapproving stare.

"Tell me about your time at Millar's Hotel,"

Hamilton asked Mary as Mrs Swain handed him a cup of tea.

"I loved my job so much," she said with a sigh. "I became fond of James and he of me. But it ended. Camilla banned him from speaking to me and when she found out we'd met up while she was away, she asked him to choose between us."

"And he chose her," Lottie said nodding.

"Considering she was his wife and we were just friends, he had no choice," Mary said curtly. "Yes, we had an emotional attachment neither of us could deny but I told him that we could never be together whilst he was still with Camilla."

Sebastian and Lottie exchanged a look and we all concentrated on drinking our tea.

"You seem to really love your job at the castle," Hamilton said as if trying to fill the silence.

"It's not a job, I'm a volunteer," Mary said wiping her eyes.

"Would you not consider a job at The Grand?" Lottie asked.

"I applied for a job with Angus Scott but Camilla was there talking to him when I arrived for my interview. She caused a scene." Mary took a sip of her tea. "I was so embarrassed. I didn't get the job and later someone told me that they overheard Mr Scott saying that he didn't want any drama." She laughed. "A fine thing for him to say considering what happened between him and Camilla."

"Funny, I can't see that pair together," Mrs Swain

said. "Angus has always been so caring and protective of his poor wife."

"James caught them kissing. He saw it with his own eyes." Mary turned to me. "Camilla has a history with Mr Scott from when she worked there. James thought she hadn't let go." She moved a strand of hair from her forehead.

"You work at The Branden Arms?" Hamilton asked.

"Yes, the pay is good," Mary said.

"Isn't that Simon Crow's pub?" I asked, wondering if there was a connection.

She shook her head. "He doesn't own it but he's there a lot. He's got a room out the back."

"He lives there?" I asked.

"No. He uses the room for…" She paused. "Business." She gave a distasteful look.

"Shady character by all accounts," Hamilton said.

"I have nothing to do with him," Mary said. "I was told by the pub landlady, Mrs Kerr, not to look him in the eye. He keeps himself to himself. But Mrs Kerr is very protective of her female staff. He knows not to touch us. She assured me of that when I joined."

"If he crosses the line, she'll likely terminate their arrangement," Sebastian said, looking up from his book.

"She must be a formidable woman," I said. "To stand up to Crow."

"Did Crow have anything to do with James Millar?" I asked, not allowing her to leave the topic.

"I wouldn't know." Mary looked nervous. I guessed

that the answer was 'yes' but I'd learned through my previous investigation that no one spoke ill of Simon Crow.

"We both said earlier that we thought it was probably him that killed James Millar," Mrs Swain said, clearly not bothered about mentioning Crow's name. "Nasty piece of work."

"Mrs Swain," Mary hissed.

"Oh yeah, don't repeat that," Mrs Swain said. "Not that I'm scared of him. I knew his mother and slapped his legs a couple of times when he was a kid, right rascal he was. Mind you, rumour was that he killed his mother, too."

"That's enough," Mary snapped. "And not true."

Sebastian and Lottie exchanged a look and then Sebastian went back to his reading.

"Did you see Thomas in The Branden Arms last night?" I asked Mary, knowing that Thomas was in there as Norma had spotted him when she went in with Breckon.

She pushed another hair from her forehead. "I didn't go in. I was too upset. I've served Thomas a couple of times but I'm not sure whether he knows who I am. But he will today."

"Why?" I asked.

"I've been invited to the will reading. The solicitor called me to say I'm a beneficiary." She took in another shuddery breath.

My chest filled with dread. *James has left something to*

Mary? I thought. I just hoped the *something* wasn't the hotel.

Mary burst into tears. "James loved me, I know he did." She looked up. "Even if he was unable to tell me at the castle. If he met someone there, as you suggested, maybe he was still waiting for me to finish, to let me know that he wanted us to have a future together."

"I think we've taken up enough of your time," I said, feeling that I wanted to have a quiet moment before the will reading. Whilst I would have liked to have asked further questions about her relationship with James, I decided to leave that to when Mary was feeling stronger and when we knew the contents of the will.

Prince came into the room and bounded up to Mrs Swain for a stroke.

"Will you wait for me to get ready?" Mary asked. "I'd rather not walk up to the hotel alone."

"Of course we'll wait," I said then instantly imagined Camilla's face when we arrived at the hotel with James's mistress.

As soon as Mary disappeared from the room, Mrs Swain sat back in her chair. "Well, I knew she was having an affair with the man. But really, I can assure you I did not approve. The poor lamb was heartbroken when he went off to India." She shook her head then leaned forward. "But as I said to her, the woman is his wife! She reckons before he went away, he asked her to wait for him and said that if he didn't patch things up with Camilla, he was going to divorce her when he got back." She shook her head. "Some men like to have their cake and eat it." She reached for a slice of fruit-cake as if illustrating the point. "But to think someone murdered him." She sunk her teeth into the wedge of cake.

"Mrs Swain, we don't know that for sure," Hamilton said.

She shrugged as she ate.

We spent some time drinking our tea and eating the delicious fruit cake Mrs Swain had baked herself. It was packed with dried fruits and had sweet sugar crystals upon the top. Our conversation moved on to less contentious issues.

Twenty minutes later, Mary entered the room looking a lot more presentable in a smart dress and coat with a matching hat.

After thanking Mrs Swain for her hospitality, we left. I walked a little apart from the others with Prince on his leash. Sebastian and Lottie were ahead of me. Hamilton walked behind us out of earshot, escorting Mary on his arm in a most gentlemanly manner.

I felt a sense of dread as we neared the hotel.

"This is rather exciting," Sebastian said turning around to me. "I wonder what's in the will and how Mrs Millar is going to react to him leaving something to Mary?"

"It's a bit odd, isn't it?" Lottie whispered. "Mary being asked to come to the will reading?"

"They only ask those who will receive something from the deceased," I said. "You may find that Camilla is not going to be at all happy. So be prepared."

"That's what I thought," Lottie said as she bit her lip and then looked over my shoulder. Mary was laughing behind us with Hamilton.

When we entered the hotel reception, there was a large man with an overcoat and hat on in front of us. He removed his hat to reveal a shock of red hair.

"That's the chap whose hat I caught on the way to the castle yesterday," Sebastian said as he turned around.

"Can I take your coat, Mr Scott?" Breckon asked.

Lottie turned around to me with her eyes wide. "I've not been to The Grand Hotel before, but that must be the owner, Angus Scott!"

CHAPTER 7

J had taken Prince upstairs to my suite with a large bone, which Norma had given me from the kitchen to keep him quiet. This had afforded me a small amount of time to myself. I stroked Prince's fur and set the bone down for him, thinking how nice it would be to see him bounding along the green grass of Ashcombe's estate. As much as I had wanted to get away from the hall and the stress the responsibility had caused over the years, I was rather looking forward to going back. I wrapped my arms around Prince's neck and in that moment knew that I wanted the hall to be my home forever. It was still a part of me that lived deep in my soul.

Having delayed going downstairs for long enough, I told Prince to behave himself. I took the cushions from the settee and placed them on the bed before pulling the door to the separate room closed. I did not want him ruining any more of the hotel's furnishings.

Downstairs, I entered the Seaview Restaurant. It had been set out with five rows of chairs and a single table and chair at the front at which a man, who I assumed was the solicitor, sat. In the front row was Mrs Flint. In the second were Thomas, Norma Lloyd and Breckon. Mr Scott of The Grand sat alone on the fifth row. Mary, Hamilton, Sebastian and Lottie were seated in the third and I joined them, sitting myself next to Mary. I glanced along the line of chairs and noticed Sebastian take Lottie's hand and a flutter of nerves filled my chest. By not acting, I was condoning such an unsuitable pairing. Especially as I had not explicitly said to Lottie that a future union between them was highly unlikely. I really needed to have a serious talk with her about it.

I turned my gaze away and watched the solicitor, who had thinning grey hair which appeared to be stuck to his head with pomade. His expression was blank and he stared at his pocket watch which was placed on the table before him. Next to the watch were papers, which I presumed were the details of the will. We listened to the clock on the wall tick as the minute hand got ever closer to the top of the hour.

I jumped at the first chime and realised I was extremely tense. I sensed an upset was coming.

"What are you doing here?"

We all turned around to find Camilla in the doorway, wearing a gold dress and matching headband befitting a cocktail party. She had clearly intended to make an entrance.

Camilla gestured at Mary. "Get out. You're not welcome here." She shook her head. "How disrespectful."

"I was asked to come," Mary said in a clear voice.

Camilla turned away and her countenance changed as soon as her gaze rested upon the owner of The Grand. "Angus? How thoughtful of you to come and support me in my hour of need." She moved forwards and her face lit up.

He stood up. "I'm sorry for your loss, Camilla." He gave her a nod.

"I'm so pleased you're here." She smiled up at him.

The solicitor rose from his chair. "Could we all be seated for the reading."

"Thank you, Mr Dickens." Camilla turned around and pointed at Mary again. "What are you still doing here?"

"I requested Miss O'Malley's attendance," Mr Dickens said.

"What for?" Camilla said. "She's not mentioned in the will!"

"Please be seated, Mrs Millar, as I wish to commence the reading," Mr Dickens said.

"Camilla, come here, my dear." Mrs Flint stood up and held out her hand.

Camilla did as she was told and sat in the front row beside Mrs Flint.

Mr Dickens sat down and cleared his throat. "I never imagined that I would be here only four days after this will was made."

"Four days?" Camilla called out. "He made it a year ago!"

Oh dear, I thought as my heartbeat quickened. I wished I'd been saved from her reaction.

Mr Breckon hung his head. This was going to be excruciating for him, I just hoped James Millar had not left the hotel to Mary.

Mr Dickens cleared his throat and put his spectacles on. "I hereby present the last Will and Testament of Mr James Benjamin Millar, signed on the twenty-fourth day of June nineteen twenty-four."

"I don't believe this!" Camilla said.

"May I ask for silence until the reading is complete," Mr Dickens said and without waiting for a reply continued. "The will was witnessed by Dr Gregory Brown and Mr John Breckon."

Camilla spun around and stared at Breckon, only feet away from her, narrowing her gaze. He remained with his head hung low and I assumed he was avoiding eye contact.

The solicitor continued. "This document constitutes the legal distribution of the estate and assets of Mr James Benjamin Millar. I will now proceed to read the declarations and bequests stated herein by the testator on the date of execution."

"I hope it wasn't changed too much!" Camilla said, settling herself into her seat.

Breckon muttered something to Norma and she patted his hand.

The solicitor continued. "First, the testator being of sound mind and body did declare that this document shall represent his last wishes for the disposition of all property and finances and that any prior wills or codicils shall hereafter be null and void upon the legal enactment of this will after his passing."

"For goodness' sake, get on with it," Camilla demanded, all the niceness gone.

Thomas stared at her, shook his head and then faced front again.

Mr Dickens continued. "He did bequeath an annual sum of three hundred pounds per year as an allowance, assuming funds permit, to Camilla Sally Millar, his wife, to be distributed annually on the anniversary of his death."

"Three hundred pounds?" she exclaimed.

"To be paid until such time as she remarries when the allowance will cease."

Camilla shook her head. "Why is he stipulating an annual sum? I'm more than capable of allocating myself a salary from the hotel profits. Even if the hotel has been going through a rough patch."

"It couldn't get worse," Thomas said. "It's closed!"

Camilla spun around. "Don't worry nephew dear, as soon as probate is issued, you'll be looking for somewhere else to live."

Thomas shook his head and then lit up a cigarette.

Camilla faced front. "Continue," she said with a wave of her hand.

"To Ina Flint he bequeaths the sum of two thousand pounds to be transferred free of any trusts or encumbrances."

Mrs Flint gasped and then reached for her handkerchief. "So generous of the dear man."

"To Mr Angus Scott, he bequeaths two thousand pounds."

"What's that for?" Camilla asked.

Mr Dickens continued. "To be transferred free of any trusts or encumbrances."

Scott stood up as if to leave the room. "At least he paid me back."

The solicitor glared at him. "Please do not interrupt the proceedings."

Angus Scott sat down.

"To Mary O'Malley he bequeaths the sum of two thousand pounds, to be transferred free of any trusts or encumbrances."

"What?" Camilla asked. "I can't afford this!"

"Mrs Millar," the solicitor said. "Please be seated and allow me to read the will."

She sat down. "There's no way I will allow it. How dare James give money to her. I won't be able to make ends meet. We'll have to reopen the hotel tomorrow."

"If I may continue." Mr Dickens took in a deep breath.

"James, what were you thinking?" Camilla said, looking up at the ceiling.

"To Thomas Finbarr Jenkins–"

"Surely not another two thousand?" Camilla said.

The solicitor continued. "He bequeaths Millar's Hotel, its contents and all his personal possessions."

"What?" Camilla stood up, spun around and stared open-mouthed at Thomas.

Thomas shrugged. "Uncle said we would go into business together and that I was the future of the hotel."

"You liar," Camilla shouted pointing at him. "You were working on him all the way home from India. You got him to change the will and then killed James when he realised very quickly how absolutely useless you are!"

Mary whispered at my side. "He was going to divorce her. It's as clear as day."

Mr Scott rose and put his hat on.

"Angus, don't leave. I need you," Camilla cried out.

"My wife is waiting for me," he said and left the room.

I wished that I could follow. Lottie and Sebastian stared frontwards as if watching a show at Branden Bay Music Hall.

"Camilla, dear," Mrs Flint said putting an arm around her shoulders.

She shrugged her off. "And you get more than me too?" She pointed to Mary. "And you – you leech." She burst into tears. "I don't understand." Camilla turned to Breckon and pointed at him. "You knew about this?"

"I'm sorry, Mrs Millar, I was unable to tell you," Mr Breckon said.

The solicitor collected the will and placed it into a

briefcase. "I will be in touch in regard to probate and will discuss the position with the executors."

Camilla steadied herself.

Mrs Flint caught her arm.

"Let go of me. I'll be contesting this will."

I leaned forward and whispered along the line of chairs to Hamilton. "I think we should go." As nosey as I was, witnessing this display was too much for me to bear.

"Everyone, get out," Camilla said.

We all stood up. Clearly I was not the only one eager to leave.

"Apart from Lady Ellen and Captain Hamilton," Camilla said. "I wish to speak to you both in private."

"Can you check on Prince?" I asked Lottie and Sebastian, then realised I was sending them to my suite without a chaperone. I turned to Norma. "Could you collect Prince's bone?" I shot a glance to Sebastian and Lottie.

Norma nodded. "Don't worry, I'll keep an eye on that pair."

"Thank you, Mrs Lloyd," I said as everyone filtered out. I faced front watching Camilla as she paced around the room. Beyond her, the sun threw beams through the window, a contrast to the darkness of her expression.

Once we were alone, Camilla turned to Hamilton and myself. "I want you to find out what happened to James. He was clearly duped by that young man who then killed him to steal my hotel." She gestured around the room. "I built this place. It was I who chose the architect. I who gave him the vision. I designed the decoration of every room. Chose the furniture and furnishings and all the finer details. I visited Paris for the most exquisite pieces. The hotel was more mine that James's – even if it was his money that paid for it. This hotel is me. It's my child, the baby I could never have." She dabbed her eyes with her handkerchief.

"I can see how much it means to you," I said.

"Exactly, I can't have Thomas take it from me like that. A will that was made just four days ago?" She shook her head. "James had said to me the day he died, indeed just before he left, the last moment I saw him. He said that he had made a dreadful mistake and would rectify it. That we would bring the hotel back to life… together. When I asked what the mistake was, he said not to worry about it, it would be resolved. Then he kissed me." She touched her lips then looked at me. "It must have been his will. He had made a mistake changing it after a silly argument we'd had." She gestured to the now empty table where Mr Dickens had sat. "Do you think I will be able to contest it?"

"You should consult a decent solicitor," Hamilton said. "Is there another in town besides Mr Dickens?"

Camilla sighed. "I'll have to go further afield. Bristol or maybe Bath to find a suitable one."

"So you think Mr Millar changed his will following an argument?" I asked. "Did something happen between you?"

She sighed and sat down. "We were getting on so

well in India. It was like the early days of our relationship. I thought we had put our differences behind us. Then we had a blazing row as soon as we got back. We didn't speak for a day or so. During that time, Thomas must have been poisoning James's mind." She looked at me. "He was always buttering him up, saying how he related to him so much more than his own father." She shook her head. "Thomas's father is much older. James was only fifteen years older than Thomas." She wiped her eyes. "We had some special memories before he died. And now Thomas is trying to ruin it all. I will certainly contest the will." She stood up. "It can't be right. I knew that Thomas was up to something. You will investigate how James died, won't you?" she asked us both.

"Of course," I said.

"We'll do whatever we can to help," Hamilton said.

Camilla slumped to the chair again and wept. "I don't know who to trust."

Mrs Flint returned to the room. "I have some brandy for you, dear." She gestured to the door. "Sergeant Chambers is here to see you."

Chambers stepped into the room. "I'm sorry, Mrs Millar, if this is an inconvenient moment. But I would like to inform you that I am officially investigating your husband's death."

"I'm not surprised," Camilla said. "I'm sure he was murdered. And I'll save you some work, it was Thomas Jenkins. When will Scotland Yard be arriving?" she asked.

"They're concentrating on the Vigilante Slasher case as the man is still at large," Chambers said.

"They'll have their job cut out tracking down the Slasher," Hamilton said.

"They have a serial killer on their hands," Sergeant Chambers said. "And he must be caught. Inspector Stone is onto a new lead."

"Really?" Hamilton asked. "What would that be?"

"If I knew, Captain, I would not be able to say. But they believe they are one step closer to catching the man."

"I've been following the case with interest," Hamilton said. "The Slasher certainly remains elusive."

"Inspector Stone has asked me to proceed with the case locally and to provide a daily report on our investigation into Mr Millar's death until he decides how we should move forward."

"So Scotland Yard are wasting their time looking for a man who kills bad people whilst ignoring the murder of my husband? A good and innocent man? It's ridiculous," Camilla said.

Personally, I felt a wave of relief that Inspector Stone wouldn't be coming to Branden Bay and hoped he would remain in Bristol.

"Would you like us to provide you with our statements?" I asked.

"Yes, I will take yours now." Chambers turned and addressed Camilla. "I will visit again tomorrow. I can see you're distressed."

By this time Camilla's hair was untidy from where

she had run her hands through it. Her head band was skewed, her makeup was smeared and her eyes were red.

"Thank you, Sergeant," Camilla said, adjusting her headband. "I really do need to go to my room."

Camilla left the Seaview Restaurant with Mrs Flint and Hamilton and I sat at a table with Chambers who took out his notebook. "So, tell me what happened in your own words."

"Lady Ellen and I heard a cry," Hamilton said. "We thought nothing of it, then when we went outside, we saw a small crowd had formed."

"Miss Penny and Lord Garthorn soon joined us," I said. "Followed shortly afterwards by Mary O'Malley. Mary then approached the crowd and shouted out with much distress."

"I approached the body," Hamilton said. "And upon checking for a pulse, confirmed that James Millar was dead."

"Did you see Mr Millar at the castle prior to his death?"

"No," I replied.

"Or anyone else?"

"There were a few people at the castle, but none that I recognised," Hamilton said. "Just the usual tourists."

"Although, on the way up Mr Angus Scott passed us halfway up Castle Road," I said.

"Mr Scott of The Grand Hotel?" Chambers asked with his eyebrows raised.

"Yes. And he's a beneficiary of the will," I added.

"I thought he and James Millar hated each other," Chambers said with genuine surprise. "How much did he get?"

"Two thousand pounds," Hamilton said.

"People have killed for a lot less," Chambers said as he made a note of this.

"So why do you think this was a murder, rather than an accident?" I asked.

Chambers looked at me as if deciding whether to divulge the details, before taking a deep breath. "An eyewitness heard his voice carried on the wind." He turned back the pages of his notebook. "They said they heard Mr Millar cry out, 'No, keep away from me. Are you mad?' They looked up and Mr Millar was facing away from the edge, then fell backwards as if pushed."

"Who saw that?" I asked.

"A visitor from Wales. They didn't know him but found the experience most stressful and have returned home."

"That's pretty conclusive," Hamilton said.

Chambers nodded with a grim expression upon his face.

"We have to inform you," Hamilton said to Chambers. "That Mrs Millar has asked Lady Ellen and myself to investigate the matter."

"And why would she do that?" Chambers asked with surprise, looking from Hamilton to me.

"James Millar left the hotel and all of its contents to his nephew Thomas Jenkins," I said. "And not to

Camilla. That's why she thinks he's to blame. Because she told us that before his death, Mr Millar told her that he had made a terrible mistake which he needed to rectify. He'd only changed his will a few days previously, so she thinks he was going to change it back to the original, which left the hotel and contents to Mrs Millar."

"Is that so?" The sergeant made a note of this. "If you don't mind me asking – other than Mr Scott and Mr Jenkins, who else benefited from the will?"

"Mrs Ina Flint, Mary O'Malley and of course a little went to Mrs Millar," I said.

Hamilton updated the sergeant on the amounts involved.

"Interesting," Chambers said. "Retuning to the day of the death. Did you see Simon Crow or anyone that could resemble him up at the castle?"

"Do you think that man is involved?" Hamilton asked.

"It's a routine question," he replied. "In Branden Bay, where there's a crime, Crow is often close by."

I guessed the local crime lord was always going to come up in police investigations but I wondered whether James Millar had dealings with Crow and decided to ask that question next time I saw Camilla. Although I would not interview Mr Crow. I knew not to approach the man.

Chambers closed his notebook. "I'm sure I don't have to let you know that I would prefer you not to conduct an amateur investigation. No matter how much Mrs Millar pressurises you. This death was no suicide and you could put yourselves in grave danger if the killer realises you're attempting to sniff them out."

"Noted, Sergeant," I said with little conviction.

CHAPTER 8

I had taken Prince for a walk to the High Street, wanting a little time to myself. When at the hall I spent much time alone with my dog walking the estate and I missed that. After purchasing a new notebook to record our investigation, I headed back to the hotel and once in my suite found Hamilton, Lottie and Sebastian eagerly awaiting my arrival. Prince settled on the rug in front of the unlit fire to chew a fresh bone that Norma had delivered. He was being thoroughly spoilt.

Sebastian had called Gosford Hall and advised them of his illness and that he would return as soon as he felt well enough to travel. I had forgotten to check with Sergeant Chambers whether Sebastian was free to leave, which I was sure he was, but I knew the young man wanted to remain and help us with the sleuthing.

"Let's fill in the notebook," I said to Lottie, handing it to her.

She beamed at me and opened it up. "I'll list the suspects," she said.

"The person in closest proximity to James Millar when he died was Mary O'Malley," I said.

"She seemed to have a genuine fondness for James," Hamilton said. "She cried so hard when he died. Surely we don't need to add her to our list of suspects."

"I'm not so sure we should be so hasty as to strike her off," I said.

Lottie made notes. "Mrs Flint always said Mary was obsessed with Mr Millar. That she was bad news."

"He was the one who was married. The chap should have known better," Hamilton said.

"Turning now to Mrs Flint, who was a beneficiary. I don't think we need to look at her," I said. "Especially as she was out of town."

"James Millar was clearly fond of Mrs Flint if he left her two thousand pounds," Hamilton said.

Lottie looked up from the notebook. "I can't see Mrs Flint staying at the hotel if she's got to work for Thomas. He seems a bit clueless."

"And he's the person to gain most from James's death," Hamilton said.

"And is the next person I intend to question," I said then nodded to Hamilton and Lottie. "If you could ask Mrs Flint about Thomas, his history, his character and why she thinks James Millar left the bulk of his estate to him." I turned to Sebastian. "Then you and I will locate the young man himself and find out if he can tell us where he was at the time of death."

"Norma said she saw Simon Crow chatting to Thomas in The Branden Arms," Lottie said. "Maybe you can ask him about that?"

"Simon Crow is on Chambers' suspect list," Hamilton said to Sebastian and Lottie. "He asked us whether we saw Crow at the castle."

"He told us that asking for any sighting of Crow is routine when a crime has been committed in Branden Bay," I added.

"Even if the locals spotted him, none of them would admit to it," Hamilton said.

"I was left with the impression that Chambers thought Crow was connected to James Millar in some way," I said. "With Crow's protection racket – he's probably also linked to Mr Scott of The Grand," I added. "Once we've looked into Thomas, I would like to pop over to The Grand and speak to Mr Scott, especially as we saw him near the castle before James died. Maybe he wanted to ensure that the bad phase Millar's Hotel was in became a permanent one."

"Is that all of them then?" Lottie asked.

I lowered my voice. "We can't discount Camilla."

"But she's asked you to investigate," Lottie said in a whisper.

"True," I said. "But we heard what Thomas said about her. That the marriage was about to end. It's somewhat different to her story where she spoke of James Millar telling her she was the only woman for him. Of course, Mary's account of her relationship with James Millar does not sit with that, either. And

Mrs Swain said that James was taking advantage of her. Just because he was stringing Mary along, doesn't mean he still did not want to be married to Camilla. Have his cake and eat it I think she said."

"Indeed, she did," Hamilton added.

Lottie wrote Camilla's name down. "Very well. We have Mary O'Malley, Thomas Jenkins, Simon Crow, Angus Scott and Camilla Millar."

I stood up. "Let's find Thomas, to see what he has to say for himself. And Lottie and Hamilton, we'll meet you in the orangery after you've spoken to Mrs Flint." I had decided that I would do well to split the young couple up so at least I would not have to worry about chaperoning.

Sebastian and I found Thomas sitting in the hotel bar on his own at a table smoking a cigarette. Upon the table was a bottle of whisky and a half-filled tumbler of the amber liquid sat in front of him.

He looked up as we entered and sighed. "At least I don't have to pay for my liqueur any more." Then he gave a short cough.

I continued to approach him even though he was giving us the signals that he would rather be left alone.

"Can we join you?" I asked.

He nodded and offered a packet of cigarettes to us as we sat down. "Smoke?"

I waved my hand. "Not for me, thank you." I took the seat opposite him.

Sebastian sat to his right then reached forward and took a cigarette. "Thank you."

"How do you feel about inheriting the hotel?" I asked. "You appeared surprised when the will was read."

"I'm not shocked he left it to me, he told me he saw me as his heir. I was surprised that he'd already changed it. And I'm still shocked that he's dead. It didn't seem real until I heard the will being read. Then it hit me." He shook his head. "He's really gone." He took a long drag on his cigarette then blew the smoke upwards into the air and looked up as if acknowledging his late uncle. "I feel proud that Uncle James had enough faith in me to leave me something which meant so much to him. He clearly wanted to keep the hotel in the family." He lowered his gaze and then looked at me. "With a blood relative." He flicked ash from his cigarette into a circular green glass ashtray on the table. "Uncle often said he saw me as a son. I guess that's why he changed the will."

"It seems a lot to take on when you've only been here for a week," Sebastian said.

Thomas laughed. "It's not even been a week of working. We rested up for a few days. But I guess Uncle James didn't expect me to inherit the hotel right now. He was supposed to live for years. We had so much planned to do together." He looked at me. "That's why it's a shock that he killed himself. Maybe after arguing with Camilla, he made a snap decision to end it all." He stubbed out his cigarette.

I thought back to the argument I'd overheard the day James died. It was true James didn't feel that Thomas was ready to take over the hotel, far from it.

"I heard your uncle putting you through the mill the other morning," I said, getting straight to the point. I could not quite understand why James Millar would have left his nephew the hotel when he made such disparaging comments about him not being able to tell left from right.

Thomas's eye twitched. "Camilla had made a mistake and was blaming it all on me. I was in a difficult position with them. I couldn't criticise her in front of Uncle James, it made me look petty, but the woman was setting me up to fail."

"I wouldn't even know where to begin if I had to take on a hotel," Sebastian said.

"Considering so many employees have left as well," I added.

"I'll have to think about it and take advice. Should I reopen? Or sell?"

"Will you return to India?" I asked.

He shook his head. "There's nothing there for me. I never got along with my father. I was a constant disappointment to him as I had no interest in cricket or joining the forces. When Uncle James turned up I felt instantly that I wanted to come to England, especially when he spoke of Branden Bay and this hotel."

"How did he get along with Camilla in India? You were rather critical of her earlier," I said.

"They were constantly arguing. He told me that he

was never good enough for her. The trip was the make or break of their relationship. He asked me to come back here to be his apprentice. He said that he wanted me to buy into the hotel. I have an inheritance from my grandfather which I will come into when I'm twenty-five. I had the money and he wanted to expand the hotel to include a heath spa."

"What did Camilla think about that?" I asked.

Thomas gave a laugh. "He never told her and when I asked him how she would react, James said that she had no ownership of the hotel and had no say on the matter. That was one of the times he mentioned divorce." He lit another cigarette, took a long drag and blew the smoke out. "Camilla is bad news. Uncle James was generous, she won't have to work for the rest of her life. She should count herself lucky."

I had to agree there. Women rarely collected more than a small pay out after a divorce, unless they were of the higher classes. "At least she'll have a modest life without poverty."

"It was more than she had when she met him," Thomas said. "James told me she had nothing."

"Yesterday, Camilla accused you of stealing some jewellery?" I said.

"Uncle James lost a necklace which he had bought in India. It went missing on the ship. Uncle blamed Camilla for not locking their cabin door. It was nothing to do with me. Camilla's desperate, she probably stole it herself!"

"So you didn't know that your uncle had changed his will a few days ago?"

"I knew he was going to see his solicitor, I thought that was about a divorce. They had a blazing row when we got back from India. Everyone in the hotel must have heard it and he only started speaking to her again the night before he died. I had no idea at all that he'd changed it."

"Did he mention a woman who used to work here, Mary O'Malley?" I asked. "She was at the will reading."

"I recognised her from The Branden Arms. He didn't mention anyone by name but when he was drunk he was always mumbling about a sweet girl – but that could have been anyone."

"Do you know if he contacted her after he returned from India?" Sebastian asked.

Thomas shook his head.

"It's unlikely he would have mentioned such things if he planned a divorce," I said. "He would probably have accused Camilla of adultery."

"James told me about it," Thomas said. "He was always mentioning Camilla's affair with Angus Scott. That was what they fell out about last week. It was the final straw, that she had been seen with him."

"What are you going to do first?" Sebastian asked.

"I'll be asking the solicitor when the soonest time is that I can ask Camilla to move out. I'm worried she'll sabotage the place."

"Surely not," Sebastian said.

"I wouldn't put it past her. I don't trust that

woman." He looked at his watch. "I'd better go now. I'm going into town for food. I won't be getting anything decent around here."

"Before you leave," I said. "Where were you yesterday when your uncle died?"

He gave a short laugh, realising I was checking for his alibi. "In The Branden Arms."

"And I understand you have made contact with a certain Simon Crow?"

Thomas paused for a moment. "I've spoken to him briefly but he's not the sort of chap I want to get to know. I'll be going now." Thomas downed his whisky and left the room.

Sebastian looked at me. "What do you think about that?"

"I don't know what to think," I said. "His story totally contradicts Camilla's."

"He did mention an argument between Camilla and James."

"True, the question is whether or not they made up."

"Mrs Lloyd said that when he'd been drinking, Thomas was less complimentary about his uncle. Maybe I need to get him drunk to check what the truth is."

I frowned, not keen on Sebastian taking this course of action. "Do not take Lottie. I'm not so sure that being spotted drinking in town with her would be a good idea. And you should really be getting back to Bristol in case your parents are alerted. Don't you think you should leave for the station?"

"I'll stay another night. It'll be fine so long as I send reports of my daily health."

I thought Sebastian was being a little naïve and very much doubted it would be fine. I imagined he was in for a great deal of friction with his parents if he did not return to Gosford swiftly. "I can see how much affection you have for Lottie, but please do not hurt her," I added.

"I adore Lottie, she's everything to me." He stared at me and with his gaze so sincere, I felt unable to continue the line of conversation. I arose from my chair and he followed as we went in search of Lottie and Hamilton.

The pair were not in the orangery when we arrived, but we found them in the kitchen, drinking tea and eating ginger biscuits. Prince had clearly missed me. He jumped up as I walked in and woofed. I sat down and picked up a biscuit for myself.

Sebastian recounted our conversation with Thomas as Lottie and Hamilton listened in.

"That's nothing like what Mrs Flint said," Lottie said. "She thinks Thomas has been a waste of space since he got here. But she said she had faith in James Millar's judgment and that in time Thomas would have learned the ropes. She thinks that when James changed his will, he wouldn't have thought that he was going to die before Camilla, with her being ten years his senior. She's convinced it was an accident and can't think that anyone would have killed James as he was a good man."

I sighed. "But from what Sergeant Chambers said, it

would appear someone pushed him from the turret. It must be hard for Ina Flint. She knew him from when he was a child. What did she say about their marriage?"

"Fiery," Hamilton replied. "She said they were forever falling out and getting back together. But she considered their marriage to be strong and believed that, had he not died, they would never have divorced."

"What about her opinion of Mary?" I asked.

"She's on the same page as Norma as far as Mary's concerned," Lottie said.

"Someone talking about me?" the cook asked as she bustled in carrying a bag bulging with its contents.

"Lottie was just saying that Mrs Flint's opinion of Mary is similar to yours," I said.

Norma dumped her bag on the table with a thud. "That's because we speak the truth." She put a hand on her hip. "If he hadn't fallen for Mary's charms, I reckon he'd be alive today. She ruined their relationship. The Millars wouldn't have gone to India to rebuild it. I reckon she summoned him up to that castle for something."

"How's Mr Breckon?" I asked.

"He's visiting his mother overnight. It was already arranged and I encouraged him to keep the planned trip. He needs it and there's not much going on here."

"When will he be back?" I asked. I had a few questions I wanted to ask him about the will. James may well have confided in him about the changes he made.

"He'll be on the first train back tomorrow." Norma pulled the potatoes from her bag. "I'm going to cook these potatoes for the cottage pie. Where would you like to eat it?"

"I think we'll take it on my balcony and watch the sun set." I wanted to relax and clear my mind before having an early night. We had much work to do the following day.

CHAPTER 9

*W*e enjoyed a hearty breakfast. There was much food as the meat would soon be past its best and would have to be thrown if not eaten, considering there were no guests left to consume it. I decided that our first port of call that day was Branden Bay Castle to visualise what had happened to James Millar. I felt it was easier to see a situation when in the right surroundings.

The four of us trudged up the hill. It was a sunny day and had a warmth to it that told me summer had settled in. Lottie and Sebastian were ahead with Prince and I walked with Hamilton in silence as I pondered the mystery: who killed James Millar?

When we reached the castle, my eyes were drawn to the turret where James had met his plight. The four of us stood in silence for a while. Even Prince sat quietly. We looked up as if paying our respects. Standing there,

I felt determined to find out what had happened to the poor fellow.

Once we entered the castle, I was surprised to find Mary had returned to her duties and was in the central gallery. She stood quietly studying the portrait of Lady Astrid of Cleve.

She spotted us and gave a watery smile. "I needed to come up here. I feel closer to James. Now the shock has passed, I realise he must have come here to see me. To tell me that he wished to rekindle our relationship. Why else would he leave me money in his will?" She put a hand to her chest. "He cared for me." Her eyes filled with tears and she took a moment to compose herself.

Lottie placed a hand on Mary's shoulder. "I'm sure he thought fondly of you."

Mary blinked away a tear. "Maybe he was going to leave Camilla. Do you think that was the case?" Her face brightened. "I think he still loved me."

"You worked at the hotel for some time," I said, feeling awkward entertaining Mary's idea that James was about to rekindle their relationship, considering it was Camilla that had asked us to investigate.

"It was the best job of my life," she said, clearly not wanting to change the subject. "I also witnessed first-hand how Camilla and James fought. Forever criticising each other. That's why I never felt guilty about my friendship with James. Their marriage was not meant to be. And of course, James caught Camilla with Angus Scott. That's the first time he confided in me. He was so upset, being a one-time friend of Mr Scott's. He felt doubly betrayed." She hung her head. "I'll never be with him, but knowing he loved me will warm my heart for eternity." She looked up at me as tears spilled freely from her eyes. She pulled a handkerchief from her pocket and I waited for her to compose herself.

"Someone called him that morning and asked him to meet them at three o'clock. Now you have had time to think, do you know who that could have possibly been? Did you see Angus Scott here that day?"

Mary shook her head. "No, I didn't see him here."

"Did you see anyone else that you think James was associated with? Like Simon Crow?"

"No," she said.

"And where were you at three o'clock?" I asked.

Mary took a sharp intake of breath. "Surely you don't think that I did it?"

"It would be helpful, my dear, if you answered the question," Hamilton said.

She looked above as if she was thinking. "I was answering some questions about priest holes."

"Whose questions?"

"An old man. He remained inside but I saw him give his details to the police."

"What are priest holes?" Lottie asked as if trying to lighten the atmosphere.

Mary hesitated, looking at us as if we were interrogating her.

"They're hiding places," Sebastian said, clearly not liking the awkward silence. "Owners had them built into their homes in the sixteenth and seventeenth centuries to hide Catholic priests." He turned to Lottie. "Remember the secret space we used to hide in at Bandberry Hall?"

Lottie blushed. "Oh, yes I remember."

"We have a few in the castle," Mary said.

"Are any near the turret where James fell?" I asked.

Mary nodded. "I can show you." She was suddenly being extremely helpful and I presumed she wanted to deflect our enquiries away from herself.

We followed her.

She flipped a stone and a small door opened at the foot of the turret. We looked inside.

I frowned. "What's that?" I asked.

Mary lifted the item up. "It's a brown coat."

"You'd better leave that where it is," Hamilton said.

"Who else knows about this space?" I asked.

Mary lowered the coat back to the floor inside the priest hole. "Most people, it's documented in the brochure about the castle."

"The priest hole is not far from the turret or the opening to the tunnels," Hamilton said. "We'll need to report it to the police."

"The killer could have hidden here, then escaped when the commotion had died down." I said. "Can you take us down the tunnel? To see if someone could use it as an escape route?" I turned to Lottie and Sebastian. "Did you see anyone when you were down there?"

"No," Lottie said. "We went right to the end, opened

the gate and looked out to the woods, then came back and met you."

"The killer might have hidden in the priest hole and gone down after we had exited the tunnel," Sebastian said.

"There was a lot of time between when we were outside and before the police arrived for a person to slip out and escape via the woods," Hamilton added.

Mary led us down the dank, dark tunnel where water dripped from the ceiling in places. I shivered and nearly stumbled a couple of times on the uneven surface of the cave-like floor. Finally, we walked towards a light at the end which shone through an iron gate. As we reached it, Mary pulled it open with a creak. A waft of nature snaked in, and I breathed in the fresh air that contrasted so sharply with the musty smell of the tunnel. I loved the sweet aroma of woodland; it reminded me of my estate. Again, I felt a pang of homesickness.

I put my hand on the metal gate and from it picked a piece of white cloth. "It looks like someone caught their clothes on it," I said. "Do you remember this cloth from when you were here?" I asked Lottie and Sebastian.

Lottie frowned. "I don't remember it, but we weren't looking that closely."

I raised my eyebrows. I had an idea that Sebastian and Lottie, whilst out of the way of prying eyes, had been somewhat oblivious to their surroundings.

I turned it in my hands. "It could be part of a shirt, or a blouse."

"Or a long white dress," Lottie said. "Maybe it's from Lady Astrid of Cleve?"

Sebastian laughed. "Spirits don't wear real clothes." He gave her a quick squeeze.

"Oh no," she said with a giggle. "I've become obsessed with that ghost."

Mary looked at me. "It could be anyone, children often play down here." She frowned. "Shall I call the police?" she asked.

"Sergeant Chambers is coming to the hotel today to see Mrs Millar," I said. "I'll take this to him and tell him about the coat in the priest hole." I placed the piece of cloth in my bag with my gloved hand.

We thanked Mary for her help and left the castle.

"I wonder if Simon Crow wears a white shirt?" Hamilton said.

"When I saw him, he was wearing a brown over-coat," I replied remembering the coat in the priest hole.

"Exactly the case when I saw him," Hamilton said. "He may have taken his coat off if he became hot and caught his shirt on the way out."

Ten minutes later, we neared the hotel and saw Thomas come out and then turn down the hill.

Sebastian pointed to him. "I'm going to follow, he's probably in search of a drinking companion and I want to make sure I'm that person."

"Are you sure?" I asked. I had been having second thoughts about his suggestion. I did not want to put the young earl into any danger or anywhere near Simon Crow if Thomas was heading to The Branden Arms.

"Do you want me to come along?" Hamilton asked him.

Sebastian shook his head. "I'm sure he'll be more likely to open up if it's only me. I'm closer to his age." He gave Lottie a kiss on the cheek. "Wish me luck." He quickened his pace in pursuit of Thomas.

"Isn't he the best?" Lottie said. "He's fitted in so well. I think the four of us make a great team."

Prince barked.

"And you boy," Lottie said rubbing his head. "You're the best, too."

"Sebastian appears to be enjoying himself," I said. "But I hope he doesn't put himself in any danger. After all, it's a serious matter. A man has died. And I think Prince is barking because he's hungry. We'd better go inside."

As we walked over the threshold, I stopped in my tracks observing a red-faced Mr Breckon looking over the shoulder of a woman dressed in fine, yet dated, attire. A trickle of dread ran into my veins as the brunette woman spun around. Facing us, with a livid expression upon her face, was The Marchioness of Bandberry.

CHAPTER 10

"Where's my son?" the Marchioness demanded.

"Lady Bandberry, how nice to see you again," I said. I had visited the Marchioness with my father a few times before the war. It was when I had met Sebastian.

"I repeat – where is my son?" She gave Lottie a disapproving look up and down then pursed her lips as she regarded Hamilton.

"And you are?" she asked him.

"Captain Ernest Hamilton," he said with a polite nod of his head.

"A commoner. This is typical." She turned to me. "You may well choose to shun your own class, but this does not mean it is the right thing for the future Marquis of Bandberry. You must cease your encouragement. And for the last time, where is my son?"

"I think there's been a misunderstanding about my

association with Lady Ellen." Hamilton stepped forward, in defence of my character.

Mr Breckon took a few steps backwards before hurrying into the confines of his office. Any benefits he had possibly received from his visit to his parents had probably been dashed.

I had no wish to argue with the Marchioness. It would serve no purpose. "I believe Lord Garthorn is in town. He's in good health having taken a long walk." I did not add that he was tailing Thomas Jenkins and likely heading for a bar. I knew a couple of the jazz clubs opened during the day at the weekend.

"You expect me to believe that my son was ill? Was it you who suggested he concoct such a story?" She turned to Lottie. "The only sickness he has is for this *chambermaid.*"

"I'm no longer a chambermaid, your ladyship," Lottie said.

"Don't speak unless I permit it. Know your station." The Marchioness took a deep breath through her nostrils as she glared at Lottie.

"I'm no longer in your employment, my lady," Lottie said. "And you can't order me about."

I sucked in my lips as Lottie repeated the message I had been giving her for the past fortnight about the hotel staff. I had been encouraging her to become her own person, to stand up to them when they asked her to run errands. I was a little shocked that she had chosen this moment to come into her own. The

Marchioness was different to the staff at Millar's Hotel and would require a different approach.

"How dare you!" The Marchioness's face changed to a pink as her voice boomed through the empty hotel. "You lure my son here for your depravity and then show me, a member of the nobility, your insolence?" She pointed her folded parasol at her. "Your mother will be deeply ashamed when I tell her what has become of you."

Lottie's face dropped. I knew she missed her family and constantly worried that she had let them down. Her chin trembled and I felt thoroughly guilty for allowing Sebastian to stay instead of taking the matter in hand.

I wanted to diffuse the situation and take tea together to discuss the matter. However, the place we drank tea was usually the kitchen, or my suite, both inappropriate for Lady Bandberry. "May I suggest we take the hotel motorcar to The Grand and take tea?" I said, then remembered a driver was no longer employed at Millar's Hotel.

"I'll take you. I will speak to Mr Breckon." Hamilton strode towards the office.

"You're romancing the hotel chauffeur?" Lady Bandberry asked but did not wait for my answer. "Very modern, I'm sure." She gave her head a slow shake and mumbled something under her breath that I did not care to hear. "I have my own driver." She gestured out of the door. "I will meet you there." She stopped as she reached my side. "Is my son at The Grand Hotel?"

"I'm afraid I do not know where he is. However, as I'm sure Mr Breckon explained, this hotel is closed due to the death of the owner."

"Death?" Clearly Lady Bandberry had not been completely advised of the reason the hotel was closed.

"They think it was murder," Lottie added mischievously.

"Murder?" Lady Bandberry nearly shouted. "And you think this establishment is befitting for the Earl of Garthorn – the future Marquis of Bandberry?"

I shot a look to Lottie who now held a defiant expression upon her face, seemingly having wrestled her emotions and won.

"The Grand is suitable for us to take tea and talk," I said.

Prince growled.

Lottie took a step forward and reached for his leash. "I'll look after him while you're gone."

"You, Miss Charlotte Penny, are coming with us," Lady Bandberry demanded as she gestured at Lottie. "But leave the runt here."

Prince whined as if he she was telling him off.

I patted his head to calm him down. Lady Bandberry went outside and after two seconds her driver drove up in her Silver Ghost. I felt a rage burning deep inside me. Even though it was true – Prince had been the runt of the litter – the fashion Lady Bandberry put him down in made me realise that she was not only prejudiced within human society but also towards the animal kingdom. I took a deep breath and felt myself calm as I stroked his fur.

Hamilton returned and stepped forwards with his stick over his arm. "Once I've dropped you at The Grand, I will return to mind Prince. Mr Breckon will watch him in the office for the brief time I'm away." He took the leash from Lottie.

"Thank you," I said and gave him a smile. "Lady Bandberry is taking her own car."

"Don't let her bully you, Ellen," he said.

"Don't worry. It's a world I'm used to."

Lottie's bravado had waned as we took our seats inside the motorcar. I squeezed her hand as she sat beside me. I felt a strong sense that I needed to protect her. After all I had done little to halt her friendship with Sebastian and some might say I had encouraged it.

As Hamilton drove, we sat in silence in the back of the car, following Lady Bandberry's Rolls Royce. Looking out of the window, it was a beautiful day and there were bathing machines on the beach. Those who cared not to use them splashed freely in the surf. I saw Lady Bandberry turn around in her seat and look through the rear window as if checking we were following, no doubt in between intermittent huffs and sighs. I was not looking forward to this conversation. I knew Lady Bandberry would be concocting a plan to eradicate Lottie from her son's life. I'd seen it before and assumed it would involve a financial pay off. It was such a nasty business. I took deep breaths. If the Marchioness wanted me to witness this, I would not hold my opinion back. Having grown up within this hierarchy, I needed to channel the strong woman inside of me. Somehow being in Branden Bay made that a lot easier.

Once we reached The Grand, Hamilton opened the door for us and we exited the car. I approached Lady Bandberry's car and she wound down the window.

"I will check that the hotel can accommodate us," I said.

Once we were in the reception, Lottie pulled at my arm. "What is she going to do? Will she shout at me?"

"Let her say her piece, Lottie. I will not leave you alone with her." I did not want to explain what was likely to happen. I would not judge Lottie, whatever she decided to do.

"Thank you, Ellen." Lottie had tears in her eyes.

I placed a hand on her shoulder. "You are strong and whatever happens, I'll be here for you." I feared this would be the end of her relationship with Sebastian. I wished I could make the world perfect for her.

As I walked in, I found Angus Scott at the reception desk, speaking to a member of staff. Both were dressed in the smart traditional hotel uniform which was similar to that of Millar's but rather than green they wore a burgundy jacket with a white shirt. I thought of the scrap of cloth in my bag, feeling I would rather like to pull it out and check it against his shirt. I also realised I should hand it to the police as soon as possible which I had not done due to the distraction of Lady Bandberry.

"Mr Scott," I said. "We were not formally introduced at Millar's Hotel." I stretched out my gloved hand. "I'm Lady Ellen of Ashcombe Hall."

He smiled at me. "You may not recognise me as I was not front of house, but I remember the visits you made here with The Earl of Ashcombe, when my own father ran the hotel. He was always excited about your visits."

I smiled back. "Ah, I have such fond memories of being here with Papa."

"How can I help you?" he asked.

I wished I was there alone and could question him about the case instead of having to deal with Sebastian's angry mother.

"I'm here with the Marchioness of Bandberry. You may have spotted her son at the reading yesterday."

He gave a sideways glance at Lottie then back to me.

"She wishes to take tea with myself and my companion, Miss Penny, and we require a private room with refreshments."

He turned to his assistant. "Gail, is the Knightstone Room free?"

She opened up the bookings diary. "It is. I will ask for it to be prepared immediately and send a message to the kitchen." She turned to me. "Would you like to wait in the lounge and I will call you when we're ready? About fifteen minutes?"

"That's perfect," I said then turned to Angus Scott.

"Whilst I'm here, do you have any suites coming available over the next day or so?"

He flicked the pages of the bookings diary. "In three days I have a suite if you should wish to move here from Millar's Hotel. I understand they have closed for the foreseeable future."

I nodded. "The only issue is that I am travelling with my dog, and when making enquiries I understood it is not usual for you to accommodate pets. However, I have employed Miss Penny here to keep him out of mischief."

"I am happy for you to bring him here, my lady. I noticed he's a fellow redhead." He smiled.

"Thank you," I said, feeling that he had lifted my mood. "I'll let you know." I'd already considered whether we should move out of Millar's Hotel or whether to leave Branden Bay entirely. Certainly, I doubted I would be able to stay there for the remaining months as I had planned. "I shall collect the Marchioness." I gave Lottie an encouraging smile. "Wait for us in the lounge."

Once outside I let Hamilton know we would be taking tea and he was extremely gentlemanly. He spoke to the driver of the Silver Ghost and then opened the door for the Marchioness as if he were indeed a chauffeur. After, he helped us through the hotel door as well.

"I will see you later," he said to me. "Send Lottie my luck," he whispered after Lady Bandberry had walked inside and was out of earshot.

We found Lottie in the lounge, seated by the

window. The Marchioness remained standing in silence, watching the view of the prom out of the large windows, until we were called in only a few minutes later to the Knightstone Room.

Inside the room, a pot of tea with fancy cakes and iced biscuits were already laid out for us, but I did not feel hungry and neither did Lottie. Lady Bandberry remained silent as I poured the tea. She gave her head an imperceptible shake, clearly thinking it extremely inappropriate that I serve Lottie. Maybe her silence was an act of intimidation as we waited to hear what she had to say and to some extent it was working.

Once I had poured the tea, the Marchioness put her hands upon her lap then looked at Lottie. "I will pay for you to take an education. I realise that you are not a usual chambermaid. You can read and write. Sebastian taught you well. And with good schooling you could become a teacher."

Lottie's eyes widened. "Then I will be an educated lady and good enough to be with Sebastian?" A smile spread across her face.

My heart fell, realising that Lottie had misinterpreted the situation.

The Marchioness shut her eyes, took a long and deep breath through her nose and reopened her eyes as she exhaled in the same fashion with pursed lips. "Your ignorance is astounding."

Lottie shot me a look.

I placed my hand upon hers.

"You, Miss Penny, will be sent to school in Switzerland. I will pay for your schooling and your daily expenses. You will have money for clothes, chocolate or whatever else you fancy, until such time as you are able to fend for yourself through employment."

"But why would you do that for me?" Lottie asked.

"Teaching English abroad would be a most fitting vocation. In return, you will promise in a signed statement never to see my son again."

Lottie frowned.

I remained silent, watching it sink in.

Lottie shook her head. "That's awful, you can't pay me not to see Sebastian. He'll be so upset when he finds out what you've said to me."

The Marchioness ignored her comment. "I've arranged for my driver to pick you up this evening and drive you to the port. From there you will be taken by boat to Calais where you will board a train to Paris and make your onward connection to Switzerland."

Lottie stood up. "My answer is no. You can't buy me."

"Your family have agreed to the arrangement and your eldest sister will accompany you on the trip and then return once you are settled."

"No, your ladyship."

"For a girl of your class to be offered such an opportunity and turn it down is insanity." She gestured to me. "Surely your *friend* here, Lady Ellen, will confirm this is an opportunity you cannot refuse." She stared at me, waiting for my seal of approval.

"Lottie must make her own decision," I said in a

calm voice. This was indeed a generous offer, much better than I was expecting. But since Lottie's family remained within the Bandberry household, it was understandable that they would make an exceptional offer.

"No." Lottie crossed her arms.

"If you refuse, I will not repeat the offer. My son will drop you like a hot stone when he comes to his senses. Men are a different breed. This is a one-time offer and I need your decision now."

"No. And I won't regret it, but you will. You call yourself his mother but you don't even know Sebastian!"

"How dare you," Lady Bandberry boomed at her.

I resisted putting my hands to my ears and gulped as Lottie about-turned and left the room, slamming the door behind her.

Good for you, I thought. I felt such a connection to Lottie that a tear threatened my eye. It was a new emotion to me. Was it pride? Was it sensing her own hurt? Whichever it was, I knew for sure I had a lot of love for Lottie and guessed it was the emotion one would usually attribute to a sibling. I had also sensed that Lottie had left the room as she did not want the Marchioness to witness her tears.

"I hope you're happy," the Marchioness nearly spat at me. She had always come across as a formidable woman but I had never witnessed her this enraged.

"I'm not sure I understand, Lady Bandberry," I said, trying not to show the irrational fear which a lifetime of living within the hierarchy of my class had instilled in me. Trying to tell myself what I always told my own staff: that she was no different to me, just flesh and blood.

"You are to blame for this, taking the girl out of service and making her your companion! A young girl of the working classes. What on earth were you thinking? Your father will turn in his grave."

I felt rage begin to rumble in my chest. "With respect, Lady Bandberry, I believe the fault lies with your family and the girl's family. It seems you were happy for her to entertain your son when it suited, when you had not provided him with siblings of his own. Miss Penny was someone to play with. The fault lies at your door for the love they share and now you cannot simply turn it off by throwing money at her. She has morals and she loves him."

"Love? You are deranged. He's a young man, with a man's urges, and simply needs the experience and then to grow up. It's akin to drinking cheap wine so one can appreciate the port."

I waited a moment to eradicate the words screaming in my head. "I think young Sebastian is an admirable young man."

"The Earl of Garthorn is his title, I would like to remind you of that. He is my son and I know him better than you do."

"I fear, Lady Bandberry, that you have had a wasted trip. And like this town, I think perhaps you need to modernise."

She paused, her mouth opening and closing like one of the carp at Ashcombe lake after they had jumped too high and banked themselves.

With her clearly unable to find the words, I decided to fill the void. "I will not be a part of this dirty deal you wish to do."

"Dirty? That is a fine word coming from you! You disrespectful, debauched woman."

I said no more and poured myself a cup of tea for my mouth was rather dry.

Lady Bandberry rose from her chair in a waft of expensive perfume. "Tell my son to be back at Gosford Hall by midday tomorrow." She left the room and I sat alone, listening to the echo of the door as it shut behind her. I took a deep breath. I needed to push the drama aside as there was a more pressing issue. A man had been murdered and I needed to find the killer.

CHAPTER 11

The door to the Knightstone room opened and Angus Scott entered.

"Is there a problem, my lady?" he asked with a frown upon his face.

"None at all, Mr Scott. Please take tea with me."

He hesitated.

"I would hate for these delightful treats to go to waste and I feel the need to unburden myself." I hoped that if I shared a little information with him, he might share a lot with me.

"Thank you, my lady," he said and approached me.

He took the seat opposite.

I passed him a cup of tea. "It's nice to take a break. I gather you're rather busy with Millar's Hotel having closed."

"We are. And how have you been burdened, my lady? I hope it was nothing to do with my staff or the service?"

"Absolutely not. Your hotel is excellent." I sighed. "The Marchioness of Bandberry is far from pleased that her son is in love with my companion. Her attempt at banishment was not well received."

"Your companion must be a strong young woman. I gather many of those offers are indeed attractive."

"A strong offer but not as strong as her heart." I gestured to the plate of biscuits. "Please eat, Mr Scott." I felt my appetite return and did not wish to eat alone.

"Thank you, my lady." He picked up a fan-shaped iced biscuit which matched the decoration I had seen on the reception walls. Angus Scott had certainly paid a lot of attention to detail.

I bit into a similar biscuit and found it delicious. Firm yet it melted on my tongue. I paused for a moment as I felt myself relax. I appreciated the way delicious food calmed me, as if someone were embracing me. I regarded Angus Scott, wondering how to bring up the topic of the murder.

I lifted my teacup. "Did your business suffer when Millar's opened?" I asked before taking a sip.

"Yes. Mr and Mrs Millar were knowledgeable of how we ran things here, of the prices we charged. They set to undercut us and to provide those things they felt were lacking." He sighed. "Camilla was always suggesting I modernise the place and she had some brilliant ideas. I should have listened to her. She had a vision." He gestured around the room. "But this hotel preserves history and I wanted to honour that." He looked at me. "To preserve it as Father wanted it. Do you understand?"

I nodded. "I certainly do. I'm doing the same with Ashcombe Hall."

Angus looked at the wallpaper in the room. "I've moved with the times with some of the decoration, but I will not change the furniture or structure of the building in any way."

"I take it your father is no longer with you?"

He shook his head. "He passed during the war. He was a great chef and loved French cuisine."

"I remember," I said. "He would often leave the kitchen and come into the restaurant to receive compliments from Papa."

Angus smiled. "He is missed. I'm not sure what he would have made of the modern world. Once the Bright Young Things flooded the town, some of our older guests chose not to come, visiting the more traditional resorts of the South West. The mature guests thought the town too modern and the younger guests viewed The Grand Hotel as staid and out of fashion." He gestured out of the window. "Now that many jazz bars have opened so close by, the modern guests are happy to stay here. And with Millar's closing, it's now business as usual – only with a younger crowd. But I have to say, the town does not boast its previous class. We have few guests as distinguished as you, your ladyship."

I laughed. "I can assure you I'm probably a nuisance guest My dog has eaten two cushions up at Millar's." I looked up to the ceiling. "Oh dear, now I have let that slip you won't allow me stay here."

Mr Scott smiled at me. "The young people have caused worse damage than a couple of cushions. I would be most honoured to accommodate you."

"I hear you and your wife used to be friends with the Millars?"

"We were." He nodded and took a mouthful of his tea.

"It must have been odd, with you all being connected?"

"Oh yes. James and Dora were at the children's home together for a few years. And of course, Camilla worked here at The Grand Hotel."

"And you fell out when they built Millar's?"

Scott shifted in his seat. "Ever since a personal tragedy, Dora has struggled with her health. At that point, we stopped socialising."

"I'm sorry to hear that. How is she?"

"The doctor says she'll never be strong enough to cope with day-to-day life. She takes care of the house during the day with the assistance of hired help. She's been a recluse for years having suffered with her nerves. But Dora was never happy seeing James, anyway."

"Why not?" I asked.

"He reminded her of her childhood. It was far from rosy." He sighed.

"I heard that James did not appreciate your friendship with Camilla?" I thought it best to speak with much tact, not wanting to sound as if I was accusing the man of adultery.

"It was more of a misunderstanding. I'd spent the day looking for Dora and confided in Camilla. Although Dora lives like a recluse, she sometimes wanders off, especially when she's had a bad dream."

I wondered whether her nightmares were similar to Hamilton's. He'd had awful night terrors following the horrors he'd witnessed in the war.

"Dora was safely back home. I came here and Camilla had come to see me after she had warred with James. I opened a bottle of wine and we both needed to wind down. We put our differences aside that evening and it was just like the old days, when we were a team and the best of friends. Camilla said how much she missed me." He looked at me. "I have to be honest, I'd missed her too. We had both worked together since leaving school." He shook his head. "The kiss had barely happened when James stormed in. He was livid, and rightly so." He sat back in his seat. "My wife is the only woman I want to be with. I would hate for her to hear of it. If she found out that I had been so foolish and indiscreet, it would kill her. She often says to me, if it were not for me she would end it all." He sighed. "That is one benefit of her being a recluse, she's sheltered from unsavoury events. She has no knowledge of what is going on in the outside world, or the unfortunate death of James Millar. If I tell her it will rake everything up again."

"What will it rake up?"

He hesitated, but I sensed his need to talk to me overwhelmed him. "A child from the children's home died. At the castle. He fell. It was an accident but Dora blamed herself – she was only ten at the time." He sighed. "I want my wife to be happy and we're happy in our own world. The one we create at home."

"It must be an awful strain for you," I said. "Running such an esteemed hotel and caring for your wife?"

He sat forward and placed his empty cup on the table. "I'm fortunate compared to Dora. And James has died. Whilst I despised him for what he did to me, he was too young to die and he was a man of principles. At least in death he saw fit to repay me."

"Ah yes, the two thousand pounds. Why did he leave you that?"

"He always said he would pay me back for my hospitality as many times, I allowed him to stay here free of charge. Even when we argued, he used to say: 'Don't worry Scott, I'll pay you back every penny.' He was a man of great pride. And he has left me a lot more than he owed."

"It sounds as if you were rather close," I said wondering whether Angus Scott felt much regret at their falling out.

"I fully expected James to repay me. I was not going to accept it out of my own pride. But now he's died, I can't throw it back in his face. I feel terrible about his passing."

"He clearly wanted you to have the money." I picked up a plate and offered Angus a cake.

He took one from me. "Thank you. I think it would be appropriate for me to pass the funds to Camilla once the estate has been distributed. As much as I'm not fond of her attention, the hotel wouldn't have come to be without her. I admire her for that and it's unethical for James to have left it to the nephew. No doubt she will contest the will." He bit into the cake.

"All in all, it is better to remember Mr Millar as a friend," I said.

Angus nodded. "He was for many years and now all I can think of were the good times. And that ultimately I betrayed him by kissing his wife, no matter how brief an indiscretion it was."

"Did you meet him at the castle the day he died?" I blurted it out.

He frowned. "No. Why do you ask?"

"We saw you, walking up there. We know he was meeting someone at three o'clock but not whom."

He shook his head. "I can assure you, James would not have agreed to meet me."

"Where were you headed?" I asked him.

"Home. My house is situated on the top road. It's ideal for Dora. With the views she does not feel so incarcerated by her illness and we have a garden she enjoys."

"Ah, I see," I said, although I was not yet ready to accept his explanation as an alibi. I was sure Chambers would be asking him for that considering I had told the sergeant we had spotted Angus walking up Castle Road.

I made no comment and continued my questioning. "I understand Mrs Millar visited you here last week?"

"Camilla was passing. I bumped into her outside. I briefly enquired after her trip. She made a sarcastic comment about The Grand doing well since the death of Major Coltrane. That was it."

"If James was killed, who do you think did it?" I asked.

Angus drained his cup of tea and replaced it on the saucer. "I've no idea."

"Some have mentioned the name Simon Crow," I said.

"You won't find anyone around who will be discussing Crow."

"Have you had bother from him?"

"No. I knew him from school and whilst he bullied everyone there, he always left me alone due to my father. He always admired him. Crow's own father beat him black and blue. Father used to take pity on him, gave him a job in the kitchen and ensured he had a hot meal every day." Angus sighed. "Dad was upset when Simon left and took over from his father's profession of general blighter, rather than a career in the kitchen. But Crow never bothered us."

"What did he like about your father?"

"Just his presence. The way he walked, the way he talked, Scottish history and shortbread. I hear Mrs Kerr at The Branden Arms always has shortbread behind the bar. He used to do a great impression of Father's Scottish accent and make the rest of the

kitchen staff laugh when Father was out of earshot."
Angus looked at his wristwatch and I realised I had
taken enough of his time. It was interesting to hear
another side of Simon Crow and it seemed a shame he
took the wrong path.

There was a knock at the door and a staff member
entered. "Mr Scott, it's your wife."

Angus rose from his seat. "I'll come now." He turned
back to me. "As I said, Lady Ellen, we would be pleased
to welcome you, your companion and your dog, should
you wish to stay with us."

"Thank you," I said. "If you arrange the bill, I'll settle
it on my way out."

"Take your time, Lady Ellen, this room is free until
this evening."

Before returning to Millar's, I decided to take some
time to myself. I moved my seat so that I could gaze out
of the window. I noticed the shock of red hair of Angus
Scott walking away from the hotel and wondered if his
wife had again gone missing but was warmed by how
much he clearly cared for her. *Will I again have the love
of a man who would do anything for me?* I thought.

As I drank a further cup of tea, I smiled at the vision
of the fairground, remembering myself and Lottie
enjoying a ride on the Ferris wheel. The tide was low
so there was a break in the boats docking at the end of
the pier. I was looking forward to our planned trip to
Bristol and decided to bring this forward to the
following day as high tide was in the morning. I
wanted a break from Branden Bay, if only for a few

hours to distance myself from the whole sorry affair, hoping I would return with a fresh perspective.

After half an hour had passed, I left the room and settled the bill, which was very reasonable. I realised Angus Scott had not charged me the full rate. I stepped outside the hotel to find Hamilton parked outside.

He exited the motorcar and opened the passenger door for me. "Lottie told me you had remained here when she returned to Millar's. So I returned for you."

"That's so kind."

Once inside I pulled back the glass panel which separated the driver from the back seats. "How is Lottie?"

"She was upset when she first returned and told everyone in the kitchen what had happened. Once she had calmed down she became angry."

"I think having that fire in her is better than the helpless feeling her circumstances must create."

"She's worried that young Sebastian will not return to Millar's Hotel and she'll never see him again."

"His mother has left town for Gosford Hall and it's unlikely she would scour the town looking for him. She left me with a message for him to return by midday tomorrow."

Hamilton turned around, started the engine and began the drive back to Millar's Hotel.

I sat back in my seat and sighed. "It's such a difficult situation," I called out over the sound of the engine. "You can see how taken they are with each other."

"Yes," Hamilton said. "Having affection for someone

in a higher standing is something which can give one great pain."

I felt a burn in my chest. Making no comment, I turned to look out of the window as we took the path up to Millar's Hotel.

Upon arrival, Hamilton stopped the motorcar and opened the door for me.

I stepped out to find Lottie approaching with Prince on his leash. I guessed it was Sebastian she was waiting for, rather than myself.

"Has Sebastian gone away?" she asked, her eyes red.

"That I do not know. His mother has told me to inform him that he must return to Bristol by noon tomorrow."

Prince wagged his tail as I stroked his head.

Lottie smiled. "So he hasn't left with her?"

"Not that I know of," I gestured towards the seafront. "He's likely to be with Thomas. All we can do is wait." I put my hand upon her shoulder. "Let's go upstairs."

"No, Ellen. I'll wait here for him."

And so she did.

I took Prince and Hamilton and I went to our respective rooms.

I sat on the settee, took out the notebook and updated it with what I had gleaned from Angus Scott. Prince sat at my feet as I stroked his back.

An hour later there was a knock at the door of my suite. I answered it to find Lottie struggling in with Sebastian.

"Gosh," I said as he slumped over her. "Is he hurt?"

Lottie giggled. "No, he was drinking with Thomas. They got a taxicab back, Mr Breckon needed help from Norma to get Thomas to his room."

I helped her bring Sebastian in. "I think he needs to sleep it off on the bed. Let's get him settled and fetch some black coffee." I hoped that young Sebastian would remember his conversation with Thomas.

After we had deposited the young man on Lottie's bed he fell sound asleep. I placed a hotel towel underneath his head.

Lottie went downstairs to fetch the coffee and agreed to knock on Hamilton's room to let him know Sebastian had returned and to ask him to meet us in the suite.

"I think we should leave the young chap to sleep it off," Hamilton said after checking in on him, loosening Sebastian's collar and removing his shoes.

"I agree," I said. "I'll ask Lottie to fetch our meal when it's ready so we can eat it up here and keep a watchful eye over him. I'm interested to hear what information he has gleaned."

CHAPTER 12

*S*ebastian groaned awake at nine p.m. after the rest of us had eaten. We had kept the bedroom door open and Lottie rushed to his side.

"You must have drunk a lot," she said.

"Port," he said, then touched his head. "It often has this effect on me."

"Fetch him some water," I said to Lottie then lowered my voice. "I will leave you for ten minutes. You may wish to update Sebastian on your visitor?"

I joined Hamilton in the main area of the suite, leaving the door wide open so I could still keep an eye on the pair, but not close enough to overhear their conversation.

"It's a tricky position," Hamilton said. "I feel quite compromised."

"I know, part of me feels it is wrong to allow them time alone and when I see them together…"

"I feel the same way, Ellen. You've only to watch

them to realise that, as inappropriate as his family may consider it to be, it's true love."

"I will ensure I'm here for Lottie, whatever becomes of their union. When I return to Ashcombe I shall arrange a proper education for her. She has a thirst for knowledge and an ambition which I thoroughly admire and she deserves the chance to make a life for herself, other than one in service or at home serving a husband."

"You're a blessing to the girl, Ellen."

I caught Hamilton's eye. "Thank you."

Sebastian entered the room, looking a little dishevelled with his collar still undone and hair messy.

"I've asked Mrs Lloyd to launder your clothes," Hamilton said. "So when we retire this evening, I will take them down to her."

"How are you feeling?" I asked him.

"Tired with a dull head. But hearing what transpired this afternoon with my mother has woken me up somewhat. Please accept my sincere apologies for the outburst you received from her."

"It was nothing," I said with a dismissive wave. "I'm sure she's simply worried about you."

"I've put you in a compromising position. I hope I've not damaged your reputation in any way, Lady Ellen."

"I rarely mix in social circles, I care not a jot of what the hierarchy think of me. I've spent years focussing on what really matters in life."

"I clearly need a discussion with Mother. And I've something to tell you as well."

"Freshen up," I said gesturing towards the room. "There is a robe in there, so you can remove your clothes and stay decent."

Hamilton stood up. "I'll pop the clothes downstairs to be laundered and collect a bowl of soup for you. Mrs Lloyd said she would keep some on the hob."

Hamilton returned five minutes later with a tray for Sebastian.

Sebastian ate his soup and bread with much gusto.

"I take it you will be returning to Bristol tomorrow?" I asked.

He nodded then looked at Lottie with doleful eyes. "I will tell Mama that I love Lottie even more knowing she refused her offer to be swept into the middle classes." He gazed at Lottie with much adoration. "She's given up that opportunity to be with me."

I passed the notebook to Lottie. "Whilst Sebastian eats, I want us to go through our suspects once again before he briefs us on what happened with Thomas."

"That's a good idea," Lottie said, now completely happy again.

"Firstly, Camilla," I said. "She had a blazing row with James after they returned to Branden Bay. He accused her of seeing Angus Scott. Mr Scott told me today that they never had an affair, it was the briefest of kisses and last week, they merely bumped into each other on Beach Road. I assume someone spotted them and exaggerated it."

"But do you believe him?" Hamilton asked.

"He appeared sincere, but you're right I should not accept what I am told at face value. According to Camilla, she had made up with James the night before he died and he'd told her as he left for the castle that he'd made a dreadful mistake which he was going to rectify. She believes his mistake was changing his will and that he intended to revert to the original. As far as Camilla is concerned, James and she had rekindled their love. And that is backed up by Mrs Flint and Norma who both believe they simply had a fiery relationship but that deep down, they truly loved each other."

"So you think she's innocent?" Lottie asked.

"I don't wish to make a judgement as yet. But when the will was read, Camilla was clearly surprised. If she thought the original will was indeed still in place, and she was the main benefactor, she would have a motive to kill him if her relationship was – as Thomas suggested – heading for divorce."

"Yes, she could be lying," Lottie added. "And could have followed him up to the castle and pushed him off."

"And the way she spoke to Angus Scott at the reading," Hamilton said. "She seemed to have a connection to the chap."

"He said they had enjoyed a genuinely close friendship for years. It's not necessarily romantic," I said.

"So what about Mary?" Lottie asked.

"We know for sure that she was at the castle when James died. She says she had not arranged to meet him there, and Mrs Swain confirmed she was at the castle that morning and there is no telephone there. Unless they are lying, she did not make the call to the hotel reception."

"She asked us not to go up to the top of the turret due to the weather and the dangerous nature of the place," Hamilton said. "The real reason could be that she knew James Millar was waiting for her,"

"It's an ideal meeting place," Sebastian said.

"But what's her motive?" I asked him.

"Hell hath no fury like a woman scorned?" Sebastian said before biting into a chunk of bread.

"If he'd rekindled his relationship with Camilla and she's telling the truth, Mary could have pushed him off in a rage," Lottie said. "When he told her he wasn't interested."

"If I can't have you – no one can," Hamilton said, looking at me intently.

"Interesting." I looked away from him as Lottie made notes "We really need to find out more about their relationship," I said. "Someone who observed what was going on at the time. Was it a passionate affair between James and Mary? Or simply a flirtation?"

"I'll ask Mrs Flint and Mrs Lloyd for more information," Lottie said.

"Turning back to Angus Scott," I said. "He suggested his romantic encounter with Camilla was a brief kiss."

"If I may say, it's unlikely the chap would give you any explicit details," Hamilton said.

"True. I also asked him what he was doing near the castle the day James died and apparently he lives close by, on the top road overlooking the bay. He was going home to see his reclusive wife. She lived at the children's home on this site and knew James Millar whilst he was there. Angus said there was an accident at the castle which disturbed her and affects her to this day."

"The castle?" Lottie said before making notes. "What happened?"

"A boy she knew appears to have been one of the victims that Mary told us about, who had fallen from the turret. I think we should ask around about Mrs Scott. It appears she suffers with…her nerves." I gave a small glance to Hamilton. Knowing he suffered with shell-shock, I did not want to belittle illnesses of the mind.

"Is she another suspect?" Lottie asked.

"Unlikely, but we should add her," I said.

"The Grand is doing much better these days," Hamilton said. "I really don't see that Angus Scott had any motive to kill James Millar."

"Thomas gave the impression that Camilla and Mr Scott had more than a brief dalliance," Sebastian said. "He referred to it as the 'big affair' and said it was the subject of many arguments between the Millars."

"Did he give any more details?" Hamilton asked.

"He said that his uncle had a physical fight with Angus Scott."

"Scott made no mention of that to me," I said.

"I'm not surprised," Hamilton said.

"We need to delve a little deeper," I said assuming Angus Scott had played the affair down, although at the time I had felt he was telling the truth.

"Should we walk up to his house?" Lottie asked. "To see how close it is to the castle?"

"That's a great idea," I said. "Can you discover where they live?"

She nodded. "I'll ask Mrs Flint, and will also ask her about Dora Scott, because Mrs Flint worked at the children's home."

"Talk us through your afternoon with Thomas," I said to Sebastian.

"I followed him to the promenade and he went inside the public house called The Branden Arms. Inside it was full of smoke and working men. He spoke to a bearded fellow at the bar. The fearsome looking chap gestured at him as if demanding something and then waved him away."

Lottie's eyes widened. "Was he wearing a cap?"

"Yes, a stocky man with an aggressive manner."

"That sounds like Simon Crow," Hamilton said with a dark expression. His knuckles turned white as he clutched his stick. It was clear to me that Hamilton's disregard for Mr Crow was growing.

Sebastian continued. "I kept to the shadows and stepped aside as Thomas left and then again followed him. He went straight to a small jazz bar called *Cocktails*, and I followed him inside. He sat at a table so I took another close by with my back to him whilst my order was taken. After a while I scanned the room and

142

caught his eye using a little of my school drama classes to act surprised."

Lottie looked up from the notebook and smiled at Sebastian.

"Thomas noticed me and came over to my table. I acted pleased to see him and asked him if I could buy him a drink – and of course the chap said yes."

Lottie laughed. "I bet he did."

"Thomas said that he had no intention of staying in Branden Bay and that as soon as probate is issued he's placing the hotel on the market and will be off to London. He even asked if he could lodge with my parents in Mayfair."

Lottie laughed again. "I don't think Lady Bandberry would allow that!"

"He wishes to live the big life until he receives his inheritance in five years' time."

"He'll probably blow that as well," Hamilton muttered.

"So he will gain from all the hard work Camilla carried out on the hotel and spend the proceeds on drunken nights," I said shaking my head. "If Camilla was speaking the truth when she said James Millar confessed to her that he had made a mistake, Thomas may have overheard that conversation and guessed this meant reverting the will."

Sebastian leaned back in his chair. "I asked Thomas about Camilla and he said he did not care, that she was an adulterer and James was planning on filing for divorce anyway. He feels that James was a saint for putting up with her and she's only pointing the finger at him to divert the attention away from herself."

"He's still the likeliest contender," I said.

"But it wasn't him that called and asked to meet James at the Castle," Hamilton said. "He was there when the call came in."

"And so was Camilla," Lottie added. "Which puts them both out of the picture.

"Not if they had paid Crow," I said.

Lottie looked up from her note taking. "You mean someone could have paid Crow to kill James Millar?"

I nodded. "It could be any of them," I sighed. "Or Crow may have pushed James over the turret because he refused to pay danger money."

"Let's face it," Hamilton said. "Crow knows how to play the police. They'll never pin it on him."

Lottie lifted up the scrap of white cloth which I had pinned to the first page of the notebook. "Maybe this is from his shirt," she said with her eyes wide open.

I put a hand to my forehead. "Gosh, I need to hand that to Sergeant Chambers." I'd clean forgotten in all the excitement.

"It's not surprising it slipped your mind," Hamilton said. "It's been an eventful day."

I gestured at the piece of cloth. "I wonder where it came from? Both Millar's and The Grand Hotel uniforms include a white shirt."

"It could come from anyone," Hamilton said. "Or be irrelevant, belonging to a visitor who took themselves down the tunnel and out to the woods."

"And there was the jacket left in the priest hole. We need time to think and to take a break from the case to give our brains a rest." I turned to Sebastian. "I've already decided we should take a boat trip to Bristol tomorrow. As you need to be back by noon, why don't you take the morning boat with us?"

"That's a great idea," Lottie said. "I'll book the tickets first thing when I take Prince for his walk."

I was rather looking forward to the trip away from Branden Bay.

CHAPTER 13

I placed a call to the police station first thing and asked to speak to Sergeant Chambers but he was not available. I left a message with P.C. Ryan to ask Chambers to call on me at Millar's Hotel late afternoon, by which time we would have returned from Bristol. I wanted to hand over the white material and advise him of the coat in the priest hole, but wanted to do so directly to Chambers, not one of his constables. I also wanted to discover whether they had interviewed Simon Crow as I would certainly not be able to speak to the brute myself! And if they had, what sort of alibi the man had.

The four of us walked along Branden Bay Pier. The wind had died down compared to the previous days and there was a slight and pleasant breeze. Prince walked to heel and Lottie approached the ticket collector, handing over the tickets she had purchased earlier that morning.

The captain of the small ship doffed his hat to me as we climbed aboard. We located seats upon the deck and waited for the rest of the customers to board. The boat bobbed up and down with each new passenger that joined. Finally with a toot of the horn we left Branden Bay Pier and commenced our journey. Children waved at us from over the pier railings as the boat slowly moved away. We sat in silence for the first portion of our trip as we watched the coastline. To our left, we passed two small islands and as we continued along the estuary, I did not expect to feel so free, seeing the shore move slowly away from us.

I held onto my hat as I tasted the salt-tinged air, feeling the breeze gently caressing my face. The breeze become stronger as we picked up speed. I looked down at the sand-stained water, which was never clear here due to the ever moving tide of the estuary. Seagulls followed the vessel as we were taken upstream towards the city of Bristol, with the smooth hills of Wales on our left and Somerset on our right, passing wooded hills and the small Victorian town of Clevedon. Then further on we floated past harbours and piers where huge barges brought in goods from foreign lands.

We reached the mouth of the river Avon, which took us into Bristol under the iconic Clifton Suspension Bridge. Sebastian gave us an extremely knowledgeable historic account of the structure and I appreciated his skill for imparting knowledge. I had to agree with Lottie, he would indeed make an exceptional teacher. I felt sorry for the young man that his dreams were not in alignment with what his family expected of him and I hoped his mother would go easy on him when he arrived at Gosford Hall.

As we alighted from the boat, the sun warmed us and the city bustled with activity. It had a completely different atmosphere to Branden Bay. Whilst I was used to visiting Bristol, I had not frequented the docks.

"I'd better get off to Gosford Hall," Sebastian said, glancing at his wristwatch. "Even though I would much prefer to spend the day with you." He smiled at Lottie.

"How are you to get there?" I asked.

"The tram to Clifton and then a long walk, but I can arrange a taxicab for you, my lady."

"Nonsense," I said. "We can all take the tram together as we're due in Clifton at eleven." I'd booked an appointment with a fashion house I was taking Lottie to.

I found the tram ride most enjoyable, seeing Bristol from a different perspective and watching the fellow passengers jumping on and off, with people going about their everyday business. The roads were busy and noisy with other trams and motorcars. This was just the experience that I had wanted, to feel a part of the crowd, to feel mixed in with everyone else, not set apart.

Once we reached Clifton, Sebastian took Lottie's hands in his. "I'll return to Branden Bay as soon as I can. Good luck with your case."

"I love you," I heard Lottie whisper in his ear and

felt my heart break a little. A cloud was surely looming over the horizon.

After Sebastian went on his way, we left Hamilton on a park bench so I could take Lottie to meet the dressmaker. I wanted to order her a couple of outfits.

"Thank you so much, Ellen," Lottie said before she opened the door.

I smiled and then noticed someone out of the corner of my eye. It was Thomas Jenkins.

I quickly walked into the dressmakers and the door dinged announcing our arrival. I turned around and looked out of the window in just enough time to see Thomas enter *Bond and Son's Jewellers*.

"Lady Ellen."

I spun around to find the dressmaker. A tall woman with short mousy brown hair. "Miss Elmsleigh, thank you so much for seeing us at short notice. I do hope I've not inconvenienced you."

"Not at all, my lady. It's always a pleasure."

"I would like two day dresses for my companion, Lottie Penny. Something befitting her youthful age."

Lottie grinned as she looked at the material in the shop.

"If you would be so kind as to guide her, I've spotted someone I know across the street." I turned to Lottie. "Will you be all right alone?"

Lottie nodded. "Yes, Ellen."

I stepped out and onto the pavement and waited for a tram to pass before hurrying across the road. I slowly walked to the jewellers and peered in the window.

Thomas was inside handing a purple pouch with gold trim to the jeweller who stood behind the counter. I pretended to look at some diamond rings but peered through the displays.

The jeweller pulled out a necklace from the pouch and placed it on a square of black cloth which he laid on the glass countertop.

Hmm, I thought. *Camilla was right. Thomas did steal the necklace.* The stones were set in a bright shimmering yellow Indian gold. The jeweller brought each stone one at a time to his eye and studied it through an eye glass, turning each gem with his thumb and forefinger. After painstaking examination, he spoke to Thomas who shrugged. The jeweller frowned and then handed it back to him with a quick shake of his head then gestured for Thomas to leave the shop.

Thomas's head bobbed as if he was having an angry exchange with the man and I heard the sound of his voice through the glass although could not make out what was being said. Guessing he would be leaving the shop, I stepped to the side and stood within the doorway of the neighbouring vendor. I heard the ring of the bell as the door opened, followed by Thomas's footsteps as he passed. I lifted my gaze and watched him stride up the street. His body language told me that he was not at all pleased. *Interesting,* I thought.

Once he was out of sight, I realised there would be only one way to find out what had occurred, so I left it one minute and then went to the jewellers and opened the door.

The jeweller looked up as the bell chimed. "Madam, how may I assist you?"

"Good morning, pleased to meet you. I'm looking for a pretty item of jewellery for my younger sister," I said. "Nothing too fussy, she's only seventeen. Maybe a necklace?"

"We have this attractive sapphire pendant." He lifted the blue stone on a gold chain.

"That's quite beautiful. But probably a little on the expensive side," I said, looking around the shop.

"What about an amethyst?" he asked, lifting a stone cut into an oblong shape set in silver. It was rather pretty and even though I was not shopping for jewellery I was tempted, knowing it would suit Lottie very well indeed.

I put my head to one side. "I think that's beautiful." I gestured across the street. "My sister is with Miss Elmsleigh across the road. I'm spoiling her."

"How generous of you," he said with a smile. "The necklace is five pounds."

"That's rather expensive," I said.

"There is great workmanship in this piece," he said. "And it comes with an attractive box." He picked up a box with the name of his business on the front.

Hmm, I thought. I really wanted information from the man and I realised I may need to spend a little money to get it.

"You can have it for four," he said, clearly seeing I required a nudge.

"That would be super," I said, deciding I would save it for Lottie and give it to her for a special occasion.

As he wrapped the piece, I felt I had engaged him enough to convince him I was a bona fide customer. "The young man who was in here before me, I'm sure I recognised him from somewhere. I was going to greet him but he passed me at great speed."

"Huh!" the jeweller said. "I've no idea who he was but if you do remember his name, you may like to hand it to the police."

"The police?" I asked, placing a hand on my chest.

He nodded. "I'm pretty certain the necklace he brought me was stolen."

"How so?"

"It is too highly valued for someone to bring to me. It needs a specialist jeweller. It's the sort of piece you would expect to see in Hatton Garden. It was made from unmarked foreign gold. He said he'd acquired it in Calcutta, which could be the case, but it included a rare pink diamond. When I asked where abouts in Calcutta he acquired the necklace, he became evasive. I advised him that I required proof of ownership and that was when he left. As you noted, with much haste." He paused. "In this business you have to be careful who you deal with." He raised his eyebrows at me. "It's possible he's a member of the nobility, down on his luck. I know a few have had to sell their estates and family possessions in recent years."

I frowned. "I wish I could place him." I sighed. "If I do meet him again, I'll be careful with my jewellery." I clutched my own necklace, an emerald and diamond pendant, which I had inherited from Mama. I glanced out of the shop. "I had better get back to my sister."

"Your purchase," the jeweller said and I paid him.

I left the shop and checked on Lottie, who had chosen two fabrics and styles which I approved of. I then went to find Hamilton whilst she was being measured.

When I reached the park, I saw Hamilton some yards away, sitting upon a bench as Prince ran towards him with a stick, which he took and then threw for him before returning to his newspaper.

I smiled as I approached him. "Ernest."

He looked up. "How's Lottie getting along?"

"She's enjoying the experience immensely." I sat beside him. "Lottie immerses herself in everything. She takes great pleasure in things that I have come to take for granted." I smiled at him. "She fills my heart with joy."

"I think you've grown quite fond of her, Ellen."

"I have and that's why I feel so worried about her and Sebastian."

"I think young Lottie would make a perfect marchioness," he said.

"I thought you were of the opinion that those of different classes should keep within their own boundaries?"

Hamilton said nothing but picked up the stick and threw it for Prince again. We both watched as Prince bounded across the grass.

"I fear the Marchioness of Bandberry does not have a modern bone in her body." I checked my wristwatch. "Would you like to accompany me back to the dressmaker and then we will find somewhere to take luncheon? I have something interesting to report but wish to tell both yourself and Lottie together."

As we ate our light luncheon in a tearoom, I updated Hamilton and Lottie on my observations of Thomas Jenkins.

"Camilla is telling the truth about him then," Lottie said. "He did steal the necklace."

"As he inherited James Millar's possessions, it's technically his. But the jeweller said it's an extremely valuable piece, suggesting it has a limited market. So perhaps James Millar did not acquire it in a moral fashion."

"You mean you think James Millar stole it from someone in India?" Lottie asked me.

"It's much cheaper to buy precious stones in India," Hamilton said. "Maybe that was why Thomas was speaking to Simon Crow. He was attempting to sell him the necklace and had no luck, so went further afield."

"That's certainly a plausible reason for Thomas speaking to Crow," I said. "Rather than him hiring Crow to kill his uncle." The more I heard about Thomas, the less I liked the young man. "The only way we'll know for sure is to challenge him."

"I am beginning to think the family are an

extremely unpleasant bunch," Hamilton said. "Adulterers and thieves."

Following luncheon, we spent an hour walking along the cobbled streets, watching the world bustle around us. Hamilton had spent time in Bristol and showed us some of the sights such as Queen Square, where children played.

Rather than waiting for the tide to rise, we returned to Branden Bay by train and were weary by the time we arrived so took a taxicab up to Millar's from the station. My next step was to locate Mr Breckon. I had questions that needed answering and hoped he would be able to provide the answers, considering he had witnessed the will.

CHAPTER 14

When we arrived at Millar's Hotel, we found Breckon in the kitchen with Norma Lloyd.

"Mr Breckon, how are you feeling?" I asked as I sat at the kitchen table.

"Could be better," he said.

"And a lot worse, John," Norma said. "We got to count ourselves lucky we've reached a middle age, not like poor Mr Millar." She stood up. "I've a fish pie for your evening meal."

"It smells wonderful, Mrs Lloyd," Hamilton said.

"We had a message for you, Lady Ellen," Breckon said. "Sergeant Chambers said he was unable to come today, but he'll be at the station tomorrow from eleven, if you wish to speak to him."

"I will visit him tomorrow," I said. I was eager to hand over the piece of cloth.

"No Lord Garthorn for your meal this evening?" Norma asked, looking to me then Lottie.

"He's had to go back to Bristol," Lottie said with sadness tinging her voice.

"Mrs Flint's not pleased as she's heard from your aunt." She nodded at Lottie. "She gave Mrs Flint a right roasting for not telling her the engagement with Joseph was off."

Lottie sat herself at the table and sighed. "I need to write to my parents to explain everything. I've avoided it, as I did not want to put them in the position where they knew something that Lady Bandberry was not aware of."

"I'm sure they'll be extremely proud of you" Hamilton said. "Considering your new position with Lady Ellen."

"I shall write to your parents myself," I said, hoping that this would soften their attitude towards their daughter.

"You would?" Lottie asked.

"Of course. If you remind me of their address, I will do so tomorrow."

"How's Mrs Millar?" Hamilton enquired.

"She still won't come out of her room," Norma said. "Ina's with her now. She wants to see no one."

I thought back to the time I'd lost Leonard. When all I'd wanted was to gaze out of the window and dream of the times we'd shared together, to pretend he was within the house, or walking the gardens and would be back for his evening meal.

Mrs Lloyd placed the pie in the centre of the table and we helped ourselves.

"So, Mr Breckon, I can understand what a shock you had when James Millar died, knowing the contents of the will."

"That was a tough couple of days. But Mrs Flint said Mrs Millar understands," he said. "She knew I was bound to secrecy."

"Did James Millar tell you why he had changed his will?"

"He said he saw young Thomas as his heir. Mrs Millar and he had fallen out. Mr Millar asked the solicitor what a decent settlement would be for a divorce."

"He was really going to divorce her?" I asked, rather shocked.

Breckon shook his head. "They fell out all the time. I expected them to make up. The solicitor said three hundred pounds a year would be a generous offer. Hence that's the yearly amount he left her."

"That makes sense," Hamilton said. "And Mrs Millar says they made up the day before he died."

"And what about the sum left to Mary?" I asked.

"He always felt guilty about her losing her job, blaming himself. He said to me that as soon as the hotel covered the building costs and turned a profit, he would pay her some form of compensation, to make up for being made unemployed."

"And she deserves it. He was her employer and he should have known better," Hamilton said.

"Do you think he still held a torch for her?" Lottie asked.

"I really can't say. The Millars were always at each other's throats, but they also cared deeply for each other."

"They had many a bust up, but they always made up in the end," Norma added. "He was silly changing his will like that on the spur of the moment. He could be very hot-headed at times."

"Do you think Thomas was encouraging him?" I asked.

"I doubt he's that intelligent," Norma said. "But it's possible."

"Camilla advised us that just before James died, he said he made an awful mistake and was going to rectify it," I said. "She thinks he was referring to the will."

"Young Thomas was proving to be unsuitable for the job," Breckon said. "And he was drinking a lot."

"He still is," Norma added.

"Mr Millar may well have had second thoughts," Breckon said. "But if he did, he never mentioned them to me."

"I do worry about that young man," Norma said. "I'm guessing he's out drinking again. He'll come to harm unless he wises up."

I thought back to Thomas attempting to sell the necklace but decided not to mention it. I did not want him to know he'd been spotted.

"Who do you think did it?" Norma asked wide-eyed.

"Honestly, I hate to say it but I think Simon Crow was involved. Although I shan't be interviewing him!"

THE FOLLOWING MORNING, I asked Lottie to take Prince on his walk and had a long lie in. I fell back to sleep and was woken by the sound of Lottie's voice.

"Ellen." She rushed into my bedroom as the sun peeped through a gap in the curtains.

For a moment, I was disorientated. I rubbed my eyes as Lottie opened the curtains fully.

"Is there an emergency?" I asked, leaning up on my elbows in the bed.

Prince jumped up at Lottie's legs excitedly.

"Simon Crow's been found dead," she said, her eyes wide open. "I took Prince for his walk along the prom and the police were outside The Branden Arms. It's been shut down."

"Take a breath," I said.

"A reporter from the Gazette was there and everyone was chatting and Mrs Kerr the landlady was sobbing her heart out. She's the one what found him."

As the revelation seeped in, I soon found myself wide awake. "Where was he killed?"

"In his room at the back of The Branden Arms." She lowered her voice to a whisper. "It was the Vigilante Slasher!"

"In Branden Bay?" I reached for my house coat. "Lottie, it may simply be gossip. What details have you been made aware of?"

"Mrs Kerr got up this morning and found the door open to his office. Crow don't normally stay overnight or turn up that early. She found him dead and his head was bald."

"The Slasher shaved Simon Crow's head?" I asked.

"No, apparently he was bald, turns out that's why he always wore that cap. Everyone's talking about it, but it's not been announced yet. The police are guarding the room and waiting for Scotland Yard."

I groaned. That would mean Inspector Stone was on his way. But by the sounds of it, Branden Bay would be safe from Crow from now on. Unless someone else took the reins of course. Not that anyone had ever mentioned him having a team, he had always appeared to be a lone operator.

"So why is it assumed to be the work of the Slasher?" I asked.

"Mrs Kerr told everyone it was. I'm going to tell Captain Hamilton. Shall I ask him to come up here?"

"No," I said. I needed to wash and dress. "Ask him to meet us in the kitchen at eleven. I'm sure Norma will have extra details she will have picked up via word of mouth on her morning trip to the High Street. And by then there might be a full announcement."

LATER, we reached the kitchen. Hamilton had not been in his room when Lottie had knocked so was not there to meet us. I was surprised to find Camilla present with Mrs Flint and Mr Breckon. She was wearing full make-up and looked extremely glamorous.

I settled Prince under the table.

"The Gazette have been over," Mrs Flint said. "Interviewing Camilla."

Camilla gave me a weak smile. "Since Simon Crow has been found dead, the police say there were sightings of him at Branden Bay Castle the day James died."

"Really?" I said.

Camilla nodded. "He was found dead without his hat. He was bald and no one realised he'd lost his hair, with him never being seen without his hat. Apparently three people saw a bald man with a beard and round spectacles – and a pair matching the description were found in his room. And as the man did not suffer with his sight, the reporter said they were clearly part of a disguise."

I put a hand up to my mouth as I also remembered a man at the castle who matched that description. I looked to Lottie. "The Scottish gentleman we spoke to." I swallowed hard, realising that whilst the Scottish fellow's beard was neater than Simon Crow's, they were of the same size. "So, his disguise was to remove his cap and put on spectacles and a Scottish accent?" As I mentioned the accent, I remembered how Angus Scott had told me Crow mimicked his father as entertainment for the kitchen staff.

"How did you know about the accent?" Camilla asked.

I sat at the table and felt Prince's fur against my leg. "We spoke to him at the castle."

"The Gazette said their presses are working hard and a full report will be issued today," Camilla said. "They have insider information, but the reporter would not give me any more details other than they know Crow killed James. He had to tell me that much to convince me to give an exclusive interview."

"Hopefully we'll have less to fear since Crow has been disposed of. What an awful man," Mrs Flint said.

"James hated him," Camilla said. "Crow pestered him many times."

"In what way?" I asked. "You didn't mention it before."

"No one mentioned that man's name," Camilla said with a sigh.

"He ran a protection racket," Flint added. "He expected all of the businesses in Branden Bay to pay so that he would look out for them."

"The only bad person in town was him," Breckon added. "And James Millar resisted paying him."

Camilla sighed. "After James refused to pay, Crow doubled his rate and said that James had to raise the money to pay the debt. That's another reason we went to India. James knew he could find jewellery to sell and acquired the necklace I mentioned. It was pretty pricey but he knew we'd be able to sell it in Hatton Garden for a lot more than we paid for it." She sighed. "He was supposed to be travelling to London this week. But it was stolen on the boat home. I'm pretty sure it was

Thomas who took it." She shrugged. "But it's his necklace anyway now, considering he's inherited James's possessions."

I shot a look at Lottie but did not mention to Camilla that I'd seen Thomas in Bristol attempting to sell the necklace.

"I spoke to the solicitor. I may be able to stake a claim, but he said there's no way I would ever be awarded the entire hotel and I can't work with Thomas, he is such an idiotic young man who's rarely sober." She shook her head. "I need to come to terms with my loss and move on."

"It's terrible," Mrs Flint said, her voice wavering in a surprising display of emotion. "You built this place from scratch."

"The sooner I start my new life the better." Camilla gave me a weak smile. "These past few days have been hard, but I'm alive when poor James is not. And it was because he stood up to Simon Crow, a man that the rest of the world was petrified of. My husband was a brave man." She dabbed her eyes with a handkerchief.

"Where will you go?" Mrs Flint asked, placing a hand upon Camilla's shoulder.

She shrugged.

Thomas entered the kitchen, rubbing his head. I guessed he was nursing yet another hangover. "What's happening in here? Are you plotting to contest the will?" He gestured at Camilla.

"There's no plotting but you can be sure I shall contest it," she said in a calm and measured tone, then flounced off. Whether she had mellowed to the idea of losing the hotel was debatable, but she certainly had not mellowed towards her late husband's nephew.

Mrs Flint gestured at Thomas. "You should have some respect for Camilla. She put her heart and soul into this place and you're going to throw it all away."

"Have you heard the news?" Breckon asked him.

Thomas looked vacant. "What news?"

"Simon Crow was found dead last night," Flint said.

Thomas's face flushed. "Crow of The Branden Arms?"

"That's where he was found and they think it was the Slasher," Lottie said.

"That's gossip, Lottie." I softened my voice. "They think Crow may have been connected to your uncle's death."

Thomas blinked rapidly. "Really?"

Norma bustled into the kitchen with a filled bag. "You've all heard then? About Crow?"

Relief washed over Thomas's face as he dropped to a chair. "It's true? Thank the heavens."

"I doubt the Slasher comes from heaven," Norma said.

"The Slasher?" he asked with a confused look on his face.

"I told you so," Lottie said.

"That's probably gossip." I turned to Thomas. "I take it from the expression on your face that Mr Crow was bothering you?"

He nodded. "He told me that Uncle James owed him

money, a lot of money. That as I'd inherited the hotel, I'd also inherited the debt." He gave a long exhale. "I asked him to contact the solicitor with evidence of the debt owed."

Norma gave a short laugh. "I bet that went down well! I warned you not to speak to that man."

"Is that why you were trying to sell the necklace in Bristol?" I asked him.

His eyes darted to me.

"I think maybe you should confess that to Camilla, considering you denied you took it," I said.

"You really stole that necklace?" Norma pointed at him with a wooden spoon.

He put his head in his hands. "My life has been awful since I arrived in England. She can have the stupid necklace. I can't sell it anyway."

"I think it's time you took a long hard look at yourself in the mirror and considered your future," I said. I checked my wristwatch and wondered where Hamilton had got to, then heard the familiar sound of his footsteps and stick tapping the ground as he approached the kitchen.

"Did you hear the news?" I asked as he came inside.

"No? What's happened?" he asked. "I went for a long walk this morning in the woods, trying to get my thoughts in place."

I knew how he felt. I too had wanted time alone, for the same reason.

"Simon Crow's dead!" Lottie said. "He was at the

castle when James Millar was killed, he was that man."
Lottie's voice became high-pitched.

"What man?" Hamilton asked.

"The Scottish gentleman we spoke to about the armour," I said. "That was Simon Crow in disguise."

Hamilton shook his head. "Without his hat. No wonder Prince growled at him!"

Prince gave a short bark from under the table at the sound of his name.

"Ah, of course," I said.

"How did Crow die?" Hamilton asked.

"They say it was the Vigilante Slasher." Lottie rubbed the inside of her left arm. "The Slasher found out he'd killed Mr Millar and murdered him."

Hamilton shook his head. "That'll be a rumour."

"Well, down the High Street, word is that Mrs Kerr found him with the inside of his arm slashed and his hat was taken as a trophy," Norma said. "As bald as a duck egg, he was."

"I still don't think it was the Slasher, it can't be," Hamilton said.

"Why not?" Mrs Flint asked.

"The Slasher will not be concerned by a small-town crook like Crow. No one outside of Branden Bay has heard of the fellow."

"Everyone's saying it's being reported in The Gazette which should be out soon," Norma said.

Hamilton checked his wristwatch. "What time is the first issue?"

"Usually noon," Breckon said.

"I'll take Prince for a walk for you, Lady Ellen, and purchase a copy." Hamilton called Prince to his side and my dog happily approached him.

"I'd love to come with you," I said. I was glad that the whole matter of James Millar's death had been resolved. I had no intention of spending time discovering who killed Simon Crow. I planned to place a call to Ashcombe Hall to discuss my early return.

"I'll stay here while you go out," Lottie said. "I'm going to write Sebastian a letter and tell him all about it." I could tell she was missing him terribly.

I rose from the table and approached Hamilton and we made our way to the exit with Prince following. We heard an altercation. Raised voices were echoing around the reception area and then we saw Angus Scott and Camilla facing each other.

"You have no idea the damage you'll cause!" Angus Scott's voice echoed around the empty reception.

I exchanged a glance with Hamilton.

Hamilton raised his eyebrows. "More drama."

Angus Scott gestured at Camilla who stood in front of the reception desk. "How could you speak to the Gazette?"

"They wanted to interview me about James," she said. "Considering Simon Crow killed him. It's not all about you, Angus."

"They called at the hotel to ask me for my comments after you apparently said we had an affair. And that the reason you left The Grand was because of the passionate tension between us?"

She put a hand to her mouth. "They won't print that, will they?"

"You stupid woman. They're journalists, of course they'll print it."

"The man was so nice. I thought we were just chatting whilst we finished off our pot of breakfast tea."

"You fool," Angus shouted.

Prince barked.

"Have some respect, Mr Scott," Hamilton said, stepping forward. "Mrs Millar is grieving her husband."

"She's angry that she lost this place, now she's selling fabricated nonsense." He turned to Camilla. "How much did they pay you?"

"That's private. But I'm done with this town." She gestured at him. "And I'm done with you."

"Good. I'm glad you finally understand there's nothing between us."

Camilla pursed her lips but remained silent.

Angus lowered his voice. "You have no regard for Dora or her feelings. You don't know how much it will affect her if she thinks you and I had an affair."

"You know there's something between us, Angus." Camilla stepped forward and picked a piece of fluff from Angus's lapel. "Deny it all you like." She smiled up at him. "You should have thought about Dora's feelings before you kissed me."

Angus's face turned crimson.

Camilla paused and took a deep breath then took a step backwards and looked him directly in the eyes. "If

169

Crow had not killed James, I would have thought it was you!"

"You'll pay for this." Angus about-turned and stormed out.

Mrs Flint appeared. "What on earth is going on now?"

Camilla's gaze follow Mr Scott. "Angus is not happy." She certainly seemed to know how to enrage her ex-boss. But she had a point: I certainly picked up on a certain amount of tension between the pair. Squared up to each other with their matching fiery red hair, they had looked like a couple from a tragic romantic play.

"I'm going to start packing, there's nothing left for me here," Camilla said as she flounced off in the direction of the lift.

"I'll help," Mrs Flint said, following her.

"For all her bravado," I said to Hamilton in a low voice. "I get the impression that Camilla has a real affection for Angus Scott."

"There is certainly evidence of a history," Hamilton said.

"I'll pop up to the suite and fetch my coat," I said to Hamilton with a sigh. "Was it peaceful in the woods? I feel I need to walk somewhere quiet."

"It was and Prince will enjoy it. I'll wait here for you." He took the leash from me.

I turned around towards the marble staircase as I had no wish to share the lift with Camilla.

"Lady Ellen, stop right there."

I didn't turn around immediately. The sound of his voice sent a chill down the back of my neck. It was the voice of Inspector Stone of Scotland Yard.

I took in a deep breath and composed myself before turning around and plastering a smile upon my face. "Inspector, we meet again."

"I'm arresting you for obstruction of justice," he said pointing to me. He wore a tan coat over a grey suit and a very tired looking trilby hat. He was flanked by uniformed officers.

"I beg your pardon?" I asked.

"What seems to be the problem, Inspector?" Hamilton asked.

"And you too, Captain Ernest Hamilton. I'm arresting you for obstruction of justice."

Prince growled.

"What's going on?" Lottie said as she entered the reception.

"And you too…"

"Look here, Inspector," Hamilton said. "Will you please make yourself clear before arresting us all."

Stone pointed to me. "You removed evidence from a crime scene."

"I did not," I said. "I've been nowhere near The Branden Arms. I can assure you, I've always given Simon Crow a wide birth."

"From Branden Bay Castle." Inspector Stone bore his gaze right into me and I remembered the scrap of material I had taken from the gate, which was currently in my suite between the pages of my notebook.

"Oh," I said.

"Will you please lead me to the evidence." He glared at me.

"You'd better follow me, Inspector. I would not have thought it was relevant but indeed, if the material belonged to Simon Crow, it would tie matters up for you."

I led him up the stairs and he was followed by two policemen I recognised as P.C.s Ryan and Jones. A third remained downstairs with Hamilton and Lottie.

When I reached my room, I picked up my notebook and opened it to remove the piece of cloth, but Stone snatched the entire book from me. "And now you will accompany me to the station."

I sighed. This was not good.

CHAPTER 15

I watched with horror as P.C. Ryan bundled Hamilton into the back of a police car. Luckily, I was treated with a little more respect and rode down with Inspector Stone who had merely opened the door of his unmarked car for me. I had convinced Stone to allow Lottie to remain at the hotel to mind Prince. As my dog was snarling at him at the time, he had agreed.

At the station we were taken into separate interview rooms. Split up as if we were partners in crime. I considered it somewhat over-the-top but was not surprised at the harsh treatment since Inspector Stone was a man who put his own reputation before the job and had lost face when I solved Branden Bay's previous mystery. I realised his desire to find himself in a superior position to me was overwhelming him.

Inspector Stone sat opposite me at the basic table.

"Will you please take me through your movements at the castle."

"Miss Penny booked a tour for us at two o'clock with Mary O'Malley. On the way we saw Angus Scott. I later quizzed him on this and he explained that he was not on his way to the castle, he was on his way home. It appears he lives on the top road with his wife who suffers with her nerves. You will need to check with her to confirm his alibi–"

Stone slapped his palm on the table. "I'm not interested in your observation and deductions. I want to know *your* movements." He took a deep breath. "Now continue."

I considered the Inspector an extremely rude man but opted for politeness. "We had a tour of the castle. Captain Hamilton and myself were at the foot of the turret when we heard a cry–"

"Are you not listening to me?" Stone said. "I want to know how you removed evidence from a crime scene." He pointed to the scrap of material he had placed on top of my notebook. "I want to know when you discovered and removed evidence from the castle."

"Oh, that occurred on another day altogether," I said, realising that instead of Stone wanting to find out what happened with Simon Crow, he was intent on humiliating me. But I refused to be baited by the man and continued with my cheery account. "A couple of days later we went up to interview...I mean to take another look at the castle as our initial trip was interrupted by the murder of James Millar." I gave the

Inspector a sweet smile which he did not return. "Mary O'Malley showed us the tunnel. In that tunnel I discovered a scrap of material caught on the metal gate that opens out to the woods. I took it with me so that I could hand it to Sergeant Chambers in case it would be of interest to him." I did not mention the coat in the priest hole. I would wait until I could speak to Chambers.

Stone sat back in his seat. "That was two days ago.'"

"Was it?" I gulped wishing I had taken it to the station immediately. "I was distracted. The piece of material could easily have come from anyone. It was nowhere near the turret. It was not a crime scene as the crime was not committed in the tunnel." I sat for a moment in silence then looked up at him. "How did you know I even had it?"

"We interviewed Mary O'Malley and she advised us that you had discovered a coat in a priest hole and also delivered evidence to the police station which may have placed Simon Crow at the scene. Except you didn't, did you?"

"Did he have a ripped white shirt?" I asked ignoring the fact that I had not mentioned the coat.

Inspector Stone took a swift breath and then exhaled with a loud sigh. "Considering the way he died, I would think that a wholly stupid question."

I rubbed my arm. "So it was the Slasher who killed him?"

"I'm the one who asks the questions." He pointed to the scrap of material. "This is proof that you removed the evidence to conceal it, to cover up the deeds of the Slasher."

"I beg your pardon?" I said with indignation. "What on earth are you insinuating?" I sat back in my chair and stared at him, taking in his dark hair, with thick eyebrows over almost-black eyes. The Inspector had the elements of a handsome man, yet his features were always so twisted that he appeared ogre-like.

"You're covering for the Vigilante Slasher," he said. "Admit it."

"That's ridiculous. You believe I'm in cahoots with a serial killer?" Inspector Stone was clearly desperate in his hunt for the Slasher if he was pointing the finger at me. "Who on earth do you think the Slasher is?" I asked.

As he stared at me for a long moment, I remembered the way they'd bundled Hamilton into the police car ahead of me.

"Surely not!" I said. "You don't seriously consider Captain Ernest Hamilton, a man that served King and country and bore the mental scars of war, is on a killing spree?"

"We're checking his alibis for all of the murders."

I shook my head. "You really are clutching at straws, Inspector."

"I'll have my eye on both of you."

I shut my eyes. This was an endless nightmare. Just when I thought the case of who had killed James Millar had been solved, albeit not by myself, Hamilton was in grave danger as Inspector Stone thought he was a serial killer? I opened my eyes. "You have nothing on Captain Hamilton, as you well know. As far as his alibi last night is concerned, he played cards with Mr Breckon and Mrs Lloyd then retired to bed."

"Did you share that bed?" Stone asked.

"How dare you!" I took a deep breath to calm myself. "We do not share a room."

"Then you're unable to vouch for him." He made a note in his small book. "Leave police work to the police," Stone barked. "I suggest you leave town at your earliest convenience. You need to keep out of police business. Consider this a caution." Stone's eye twitched.

I knew he was simply using this as a bullying tactic, in the hope I would leave Branden Bay. I stood up and the chair scraped against the floor. That had made my mind up. I certainly was *not* going to return to Ashcombe Hall. I would not be driven out of town by him.

"I'll show myself out, Inspector."

I LEFT the police station feeling somewhat shaky and saw the Gazette was on sale. The headline stated: *Vigilante Slasher Strikes Again*. I reached for a coin and purchased a copy, wondering why the press and police had concluded that the Vigilante Slasher had killed Simon Crow. I read the newspaper as I walked down the slope of the High Street towards the promenade. I longed to take deep breaths on the beach, to blow away the feeling of being interrogated by the awful Inspector. The newspaper report stated that sources suggested Simon Crowborough, known locally as Simon Crow, had pushed James Millar from the turret and that The Vigilante Slasher had taken revenge. I read on, discovering that the reason they thought it was the Vigilante Slasher was that Crow's hat had been stolen as a trophy and a cross had been etched into his inner arm. *Just as Lottie said,* I thought.

I pulled a face and lowered the paper for a moment. *Could the Vigilante Slasher really have killed Simon Crow?* Maybe Crow had bragged of the murder to contacts in Bristol, after all it was not that far from Branden Bay. The Slasher might have heard about the way Crow terrorised the locals. I shuddered. Whatever had occurred, the police appeared to be satisfied that Simon Crow had killed James Millar. I felt rather flat and chastened myself, knowing it was because I had wanted to be the one to solve the murder. I had not been at all bothered earlier on in the day, I was merely relieved the murder had been solved, until the Inspector was so rude to me. I realised I really should not let the man get under my skin.

"Ellen." I swung around to find Hamilton striding up to me with his stick over his arm.

"Thank goodness they let you out," I said.

"What do you think?" he asked.

"About what?"

"Who murdered James Millar and Crow?"

I lifted the newspaper and tapped it. "Crow killed James and the Vigilante Slasher took revenge."

Hamilton took the newspaper from me. "This is all wrong."

"Not according to Inspector Stone."

"And where's your notebook? Did he return it to you?"

I shook my head. "Maybe they think it'll have some sort of clue as to who the Slasher is. I have to warn you, Stone rather thinks it's you." I gave a small laugh with a dismissive wave. "He said he's checking all of your alibis for the murders but don't worry, the Inspector is a fool."

"He's playing with you. He didn't even speak to me about it," Hamilton said. "He left Chambers to interview me." He looked around and directed me to the doorway of a closed restaurant. "Chambers let something slip. They don't think it was the Slasher who killed Crow, they think it was a copycat."

"Are you sure?" I put my hand to my mouth.

He nodded.

"So we could be looking at one killer, who killed James and then Crow, making it look as if it was the Slasher?" I opened my eyes wider.

"The police think someone paid Crow to kill James Millar and that Crow was either asking for more money or blackmailing them. So they killed them, leaving the scene to look as if it was the Vigilante Slasher."

"It must have been someone strong to kill Crow."

"Chambers said Stone is making no effort to tell the public that it wasn't the Slasher, as he wants the case tied up so he can get back to hunting for the real serial killer."

"I guess he doesn't care about a small murder in a small town," I said.

Hamilton nodded. "Correct, Chambers said they were asked to keep it hush-hush. Blame it on the Slasher and it's another case solved. Stone is hoping the real Slasher may be coaxed out into the open to dispute the matter."

I knew Sergeant Chambers was not fond of Stone. "Chambers probably told you so we can keep our ears to the ground when he cannot."

"He asked me to update him on anything we discover."

"I'm guessing the Vigilante Slasher is probably still in Bristol. I wonder if he'll mind being blamed for the death?" I pondered.

"I'm sure he will not feel baited, he'll be one step ahead, that's for sure."

"So, how do they know it's a copycat?" I asked.

"Unfortunately, Chambers would not divulge that information. If I revealed it, he would be in trouble with Stone." He checked his wristwatch. "I have a meeting with the bank in Bristol. I still have time to catch the afternoon train."

CHAPTER 16

hen I returned to my suite, I found Lottie writing. Prince stood up from the rug and greeted me with much enthusiasm. As I brought her up to date, it was clear that Lottie missed Sebastian.

"Let's go to the kitchen, you ate nothing at breakfast," I said to her.

"I don't want any food," she said.

"You'll feel better with something in your stomach. Now come along."

She reluctantly pulled herself to standing.

When we arrived in the kitchen, we found Norma wiping the worktop. "There you are. What were all those shenanigans about?"

I gave a dismissive wave. "Inspector Stone was attempting to drive me out of town."

"That man is a menace. At least he didn't keep you

in." She took a sharp intake of breath. "They've not flung the captain in the cells, have they?"

"No, he has some business to attend to and has taken the train to Bristol."

"Me and John are going out tonight. With this nasty business solved, we're having a drink to reminisce over Mr Millar. As for Simon Crow, he got his comeuppance. He was a bad lot to kill someone like James, so respected in the community." She sighed. "We don't know what we're going to do when the food runs out. Or what's to become of us."

"If you're worried and want contacts, do not be afraid to ask. And I will of course give you both glowing letters of recommendation."

Lottie sat at the table in silence, staring at her hands.

"Thank you, my lady." Norma gestured to the larder. "We've cheese and cold meats and there's bread and tomatoes if you want me to make you something?"

"We'll be fine to do that ourselves," I said. "Have a relaxing afternoon and prepare for your evening out with Mr Breckon."

"Thank you, my lady. I think I'll go to one of the guest rooms with a large bathtub and have a soak."

"I don't blame you," I said as she left the room.

Lottie stood up and slowly walked to the larder.

"Sit down, my dear. I'll fetch it." I found bread, cheese and pickles and placed them on the table. "It's like a ghost ship here. To think that only a few weeks ago, this hotel was busy and fully booked. It's so sad."

Lottie simply nodded. I felt that this was the perfect time for me to have that awkward discussion about Sebastian.

I buttered her a slice of bread, cut a wedge of cheese and put it upon the plate in front of her. "What are your thoughts?" I asked her.

"I'm worried I'll never see him again. Normally he writes to me every day and I've not received anything today." Tears ran down her cheeks.

"I have no doubt that he truly loves you and his heart is most definitely yours." I took a deep breath. "But the responsibility which accompanies his position in society will weigh heavily upon him as he grows."

Lottie pulled her handkerchief out and wiped her cheeks.

"When Papa died, the responsibility was overwhelming," I said. "I was only young and I had the hall and estate to look after."

"But you had your husband."

"We had only recently begun our courting. I did not know where it would lead, even though I wished us to be together. It's not only the building and land you inherit, it's the staff, the people whose livelihoods depend on you. The money they earn from your land and from running your house is needed to support their families."

"But he doesn't want any of that," Lottie said, wringing her hands. "He wants to be a teacher. That's noble. He wants to open a school to teach children of the working classes, he said we can run it together to give them a better chance in life."

My heart went out to the young man. "He's a good man with a good heart. I'm simply making you aware of the responsibility that will weigh heavily on him. As much as he loves you, his wish to follow his heart may appear selfish when presented with his inheritance."

Lottie sobbed and I felt dreadful. I moved along the bench towards her and put my arm around her. "I'm not attempting to upset you. It would be unkind of me not to explain how I felt about the hall. That it is in my blood and that I must serve it until my dying day." I had not realised how strong the feeling was until I had come to Branden Bay. "As hard as it is."

"I'm not giving up on him, Ellen."

I pushed her hair away from her face. "I wouldn't ask you to, but my conscience is such that I feel compelled to explain my fears. And when we return to Ashcombe, I will ensure you receive the education you deserve."

She blinked away the tears. "Thank you, Ellen."

"Now eat up. You can either come for a walk with me and Prince or do as Mrs Lloyd is and take a long hot bath."

"I want to stay at the hotel, Ellen. To see if a letter comes."

AN HOUR LATER, I left the hotel with Prince. As much as I wanted to rest, I still had that nagging question in my head. *Why do the police know it was not the Slasher?* My first stop would be to see Mrs Kerr. I took the road down to the promenade but The Branden Arms was still closed. As I stood staring at it, an elderly woman passed.

"Awful business," she said.

"I wanted to give my condolences to Mrs Kerr."

'She's staying at her parent's, though I don't know exactly where that is, but it ain't far."

I bade the old lady farewell and decided to ask Mary. She would know where Mrs Kerr was residing.

I patted my dog. "Are you up for a longer walk, boy?"

Prince barked and I stroked him, feeling he was the only familiar thing in my life at that moment.

Once I reached Mary's house, I was pleased when she answered the door. After I had asked after her well-being, I brought up the reason I was there.

"I came to ask where Mrs Kerr lives," I said as we spoke on the doorstep.

"Why's that?" Mary asked.

"I want to see if she's well. Considering she witnessed a death." I didn't want to repeat that there was something off with the murder, not wanting to alert anyone to the fact and put Chambers into an awkward position with Stone for spilling the beans to Hamilton.

"She's staying with her parents. Just up the road, Number forty-five, it's not far away from here. I'll show you. I'm about to go up to the castle, anyway."

I waited for her as Prince sniffed the bushes.

I chatted away to Mary as we made our way further up Castle Road. The weather was changing to match my mood. As we rounded the curve in the road, we saw Inspector Stone coming out of a house. I let Prince sniff bushes in someone's front garden. The Inspector did not look down the road at us and he and a uniformed officer got into the police car, turned it around and then drove down the hill. I looked away and, with Prince in the bushes, I hoped he had not spotted us.

"They've came out of Mrs Kerr's parent's house," Mary said.

"I'll come up to the castle afterwards and see you there," I said.

"Do you want me to take your dog?" she asked.

I looked at her and then to Prince.

He barked and whilst I was nervous about letting him go, I knew I would have a better chance of being allowed in to see Mrs Kerr if I did not have him with me.

"Thank you. I won't be long," I said.

"Come along, boy," Mary took his leash.

I knocked on the door. Mrs Kerr's mother answered, looking none too pleased at the prospect of another visitor. "Yes?" She gave me a look up and down.

"Lady Ellen of Ashcombe Hall, to see Mrs Kerr of The Branden Arms." Sometimes having a title was an advantage as she soon stepped aside.

"I'll let her know you are here." She returned within a matter of seconds. "Do come through to my front room," she said with a smile. "Mabel is in there."

I went into the room to find Mrs Kerr seated by the window. The room was not dissimilar to Mrs Swain's however was decorated in red, rather than green.

"I'm so sorry to intrude. I wanted to extend my condolences as I understand you lost a dear friend earlier today who died at the hands of the Vigilante Slasher?"

"Do take a seat, my lady." She put a handkerchief up to her face. "He wasn't a popular man but was always good to me. And I don't think he killed James Millar. No matter what the newspaper said." She sniffed. "I can't get it out of my mind. The way I found him, laying there before me, his arm slashed with a cross in it." She blinked a couple of times. "I knew straight away it was the Slasher, and he took his cap. Simon would have hated to die like that. The police still keep asking me questions about who he was speaking to earlier that week." She looked up at me. "Do you think the Slasher was drinking in my pub?" She visibly gulped. "I've been trying to bring to mind every new face that came in."

"Who did he speak to that day?" I asked, taking a seat on a settee.

"He spoke to a good many people, he was always at the pub." She sighed. "I've just given a long list of names to the police." She shook her head. "I won't feel as safe without Simon around. I never had any bother from no one. I've been running the pub on my own since my

Harold passed away. A woman needs that sort of presence for protection."

"What exactly did you see when you found him?" I asked, feeling awful for having to make her relive the experience – but the desire to discover the truth was overwhelming.

"I found him first thing, lying there on the floor, without his hat, as bald as a baby's bottom he was – I never knew he'd lost his hair. He had his arms out. I looked to my left and his arm had a cross in it. It was then I knew it was the work of the Slasher. I'd read all about it." She sighed. "I think I'm going to have to close up for good. Who's going to want to come to The Branden Arms with the Vigilante Slasher drinking there? It's killed trade at The Bell in Bristol."

I frowned. "If you looked to your left and saw his arm was slashed, would that be his right arm?"

"Erm, yes, it was."

The wrong arm, I thought.

"Hang on, doesn't he normally slash the left arm?" She sat up. "Do you think I should tell the police?"

"They will already know. They have his body."

She sat back. "Of course." She had fear in her eyes. "But the papers said it was the Slasher."

"I think we should keep this to ourselves, otherwise we may compromise the police investigation."

She widened her eyes. "I'm not leaving this place 'til they found who done it."

I gave Mrs Kerr some soothing condolences and asked after her health, as we drank tea which her mother had made for us. As soon as it felt polite to do so, I left and promised to let her know if the police made any progress.

Once on the pavement I sped up. I felt a little uncomfortable leaving Prince with Mary, especially as she was on my list of suspects. I wished Hamilton was still in town so I could reveal my discovery. And if the killer knew about the Slasher taking a trophy, they would have known about the left arm.

Hmm, I thought, *unless they don't know their left from their right.*

I stopped in my tracks as pins and needles tingled over my body, remembering James Millar's own words and a detail that I had asked Lottie to write in my notebook. *Thomas, you don't know your left from your right.*

I sped up. I needed to collect Prince and to get to the Police Station to speak to Sergeant Chambers. I would certainly not be dealing with Inspector Stone. I knew I would be able to speak freely to Chambers, without a massive ego coming between us. I had read the recent work of Sigmund Freud which had been published and was sure he would take much interest in a man such as Inspector Stone.

As unlikely as it appeared that young Thomas could have killed a man such as Crow. He might have got the man drunk and stabbed him whilst he was sleeping. Anything was possible.

As I rounded a bend in the road, I saw a man running ahead of me carrying his hat. I spotted his shock of red hair. *Angus Scott.* I guessed he was having further issues with his wife.

With the weather not being as pleasant as it had been, there were fewer visitors at the castle. I ran up the steps, eager to find my dog.

Inside it was dark and quiet. I found Mary with Prince in the gallery.

She turned to me. "How was Mrs Kerr?"

"She is ever so distressed. It must be harrowing to find a man murdered in such a way." I did not elaborate. "Is it possible for me to have a look at the top of the turret?" I asked her.

"Yes, but be careful. Especially with the storm drawing in. I'm going to walk around to see if I can find anyone to remind them that we close soon," Mary said. "I'm locking up at four."

I climbed the steps of the turret with Prince as he whimpered.

Whilst I did not believe in apparitions, a part of me worried that he could sense the ghost Lottie was convinced roamed the castle.

As I reached the top, I held tightly onto Prince's leash and stopped still as the view of the bay took my breath away. Even with the dark clouds rolling in, it was beautiful.

I sighed. "It's a tragedy that such a glorious town is the setting for a double murder. Who asked James Millar to meet them here?" I called out as the wind picked up. It couldn't have been Thomas or Camilla, they were with him when the call came in. Mrs Swain confirmed Mary was at the castle at the time of the call and there was no telephone there. Angus Scott was definitely a contender but I realised that Simon Crow was the most likely, considering we spotted him at the castle ourselves, albeit in disguise. Although I found it difficult to imagine any of them killing Crow and slashing him. It seemed to be the work of a mad man. *Or someone desperate,* I thought. I stared at the spot James had been pushed from and looked at the wall. It wasn't that high. A wall that anyone could easily be pushed over. I shuddered.

"He's dead, he's dead."

I heard the voice of a woman floating up the turret stairs.

Prince whined.

I stood still, listening until before me a woman appeared.

Her hair was long and white, she wore a white nightdress and her feet were bare. Her eyes were huge and blue and her skin so pale, it was as if she'd never seen daylight. So white I asked myself: *is she a ghost?*

She screamed, turned and ran from me.

My heart pounded as I pulled Prince and took chase, following her down the spiral staircase as the wind whooshed down behind us.

I heard another eerie wail. She was certainly fast, considering she was barefooted.

Prince howled.

As I reached the bottom, I saw a flash of white pass at the end of the passage.

Prince barked and pulled at the leash.

I had an idea as to who this woman was.

Mary rounded the bend and I nearly bumped into her.

"Are you hurt?" she asked me.

"He's dead, he's dead," the woman called in the distance.

Mary looked to her left and then back to me and bit her lip.

"Could you please confirm who the woman I just saw is, and don't tell me she's an apparition."

Mary clasped her hands together. "I'm not supposed to say."

"It's Mrs Dora Scott, isn't it?"

Mary hung her head. "When I got the job, I was to act as if she was a ghost if she was here." She looked up at me. "It brings more visitors."

"And you didn't feel the need to tell the police?"

"I never saw her the day James was pushed from the turret and she's harmless. It's not often she's here, maybe once a month or less. The police asked me for a list of the people I saw that day and I told them."

"Do you realise she knew James Millar?"

Mary frowned. "Well, she's Angus Scott's wife. He comes here looking for her sometimes. So I guess James would have known who she was. He only mentioned her when talking about Camilla."

"He's dead, he's dead," Dora wailed in the distance.

"I'm following her," I said.

"Don't go that way," Mary said gesturing towards

the tunnels. "She goes out through the passage to the woods, but it will be quicker if you go out the front door and around the outside of the castle. I need to go down the tunnel to lock up."

"I'm going to follow her to make sure she goes home, then will go straight to the police station. Meet me there."

"But it was Simon Crow that killed James," Mary said.

"Still, the police need to know," I said, not having time to explain.

Once outside, I ran around the side of the castle as Mary had suggested, with Prince ahead of me. Around the back I found the tunnel gate wide open. I looked down the tunnel and saw Mary at the end, walking towards the door to lock up. I turned round to face the woods. Someone wailed in the distance. There was a steep incline and I scrambled up the side with Prince's help as he tugged on his leash. I was pleased to be wearing comfortable shoes, although not happy that my coat became caught in brambles.

As soon as the ground levelled out, I came to a path. Scanning the area, I strained to register movement but could only hear the wind in the trees and birdsong.

Prince tugged at the leash, to lead me to the left. I assumed that was the direction to the Scott house.

"Go on, boy," I said as I allowed some slack in the leash.

Prince took us along the path as it led us away from the castle, meandering through the woods. I was now convinced the white piece of cloth had come from the woman's gown. It would have been helpful if Mary had told the police about Dora's visits. I continued along the path, allowing Prince to lead the way until he veered off to a high stone wall. I stood for a moment, realising we were at the boundary of the gardens belonging to the houses which backed onto the woods.

I heard a cry. This time it was a man's voice that I recognised.

"Dora, Dora. Where are you?" It was Angus Scott and he sounded panicked.

As I came out of the bushes, I saw a flash of white. Dora turned around to face me. She put her index finger up to her lips whilst she stared at me, as if asking me to hush.

I heard a gate opening so stepped back into the bushes and rubbed Prince's back, hoping he would not bark.

"There you are," Angus said. "Edith has had enough, she's left. She says she can't cope with you running off. You know what I said would happen if you kept escaping like this."

"I'm sorry, Angus, I won't do it again. Please, I don't want to go back to that hospital." Dora descended into sobs.

"Where have you been?" her husband asked as he led her through the gate.

"In the woods, just the woods. Please, Angus."

Prince scuffed at the woodland floor and I thought it best to leave him to it, rather than risk him barking, so I dropped the leash and moved out of the bushes. I inched along the boundary wall of the Scott residence towards the gate, which had a crack in the wood. Through the missing slither, I saw Angus Scott with his arms around his wife.

"I can't protect you any more," he said, his voice thick with emotion. "I can't cope."

"No! Angus no!" she screamed. "I don't want to go, please, it won't happen again. I don't know how I got out." She put her hands to her head. "I just don't remember."

"It's not only you that's getting hurt, now, is it?"

"No." She gave such a pitiful wail that it sent a shock of fear through me.

Scott lifted her and threw her over his shoulder as she screamed, thumping his back with her hands in fists as he carried her into his house. Her screams were no longer audible after I heard the door slam. I let out a long breath, having held it whilst I had watched. Part of me felt compelled to protect her and follow her in. She had been almost childlike. But I could not go alone. I would have to collect Prince and meet Mary at the police station. I scrambled to my feet and made my way back to Prince, pleased that he'd not barked and given us away. He was still sniffing and digging at the ground. I felt the need to take flight, to get away from that place and alert the police to attend the Scott household as soon as possible.

"Come on, boy," I whispered as I tugged at his leash.

Prince became excited and barked, jumped up a

couple of times and then sniffed the ground again. *Trust him to find a rabbit,* I thought.

"Come along." I pulled him and he stopped barking. He wagged his tail, burying his snout in the hole, and then lifted his head. Inside his mouth was a flat cap.

CHAPTER 17

I placed a hand to my chest, fighting for breath as I looked at my jubilant dog and realised he had the late Simon Crowborough's cap in his mouth, presumably hidden by the person who had killed him. I turned and looked down the deep hole he had dug. At the bottom was a knife. I let go of the leash and picked up a stick. With a shaking hand I scraped the mud from the handle, upon which were the initials *A.S.*.

I dropped the stick and stepped backwards. I fumbled for Prince's leash then turned, but had to hold onto a branch to avoid losing my balance.

Prince barked and dropped the cap at his feet.

I turned and then jumped.

Angus Scott stared at me from his gate.

I stood still, like a deer on the Ashcombe Estate having spotted a hunter. Wondering should I flee? Or act as if I was just passing, pick a leaf from a bush and casually walk away? Angus lowered his gaze to Prince's feet, no doubt eyeing Simon Crow's cap. He looked back up at me and as we stared at each other, time appeared to stand still.

"I think you'd better come inside," he called out then stepped to the left and gestured to his gate.

"I have to get back," I said and leaned down, grabbing Prince's collar.

Angus took a step towards us.

Prince began to snarl. He growled loudly and then barked at him.

Angus stopped in his tracks. I was so pleased I had my dog with me.

"I need to explain," he said. "I'm not going to hurt you. I have to..." He stopped as if attempting to compose himself. "I have to tell someone."

I caught his gaze and saw a man who needed to unload, to get something off his chest. I had seen it at the hall when it was a convalescent home. Some men close to death wanted to get their sins off their chests before facing their maker. I felt a nudge within.

"You can bring your dog," he said. "He will protect you."

I nodded and, with my heart pounding and legs rather on a wobble, I fumbled for Prince's leash and walked towards Angus as he turned and passed through the gate. I followed him down the path to his back door.

As soon as I stepped over the threshold, I heard Dora sobbing.

Angus led me to his kitchen and motioned for me to sit at one end with Prince whilst he took a seat at the opposite end. I was seated close to the exit and exhaled, convinced I could escape if I needed to.

"I've called the asylum," Angus said. "They're sending an ambulance to collect Dora. The doctor has already signed the committal papers. I was just trying..." He took in a shuddering breath. "To delay it. In case there was another way."

I looked towards the door which Dora was thumping against.

"Did she push James over the edge?" I asked in a quiet voice.

Angus nodded. "I found this note." He pushed an envelope across the table.

I caught it. It had *Dora Scott* written on it. I took out a handwritten note.

I saw you push James at the castle.

Meet me at my office, at ten.

The door will be open.

Simon Crow

"Gosh," I said with a whisper.

Angus coughed as if trying to mask a sob. It was clearly hard for him.

"Help me, help me," Dora screamed, rattling the door, trying to get out of the locked room.

"It's secure," he said. "She won't be able to get out. She escaped today as she overpowered the woman I hired to look after her."

Angus appeared distraught with his shoulders

drooped as if the realisation had sunk in. His wife had to leave.

His face cracked. "I should have committed her weeks ago, then this mess would not have happened. James would be alive, and Simon. It's entirely my fault."

"Surely she didn't kill Crow?" I asked.

There was a knock at the door.

"Please wait until she's left the house, then I'll explain."

He closed the kitchen door as if trying to give his wife some dignity as she was removed from the house. Her cries cut straight through to the core of me and Prince whimpered at my side. I found my own tears running down my cheeks, thinking how hard it must be for Angus Scott to commit the woman he loved. But it would appear she had a side to her that was seemingly possessed by an inner demon over which she had no control. I gulped, imagining the innocent-looking woman committing a double murder.

After a noisy but swift commotion, I soon heard a vehicle drive away and the sobs Angus attempted to muffle. I busied myself making a pot of tea. When I opened the drawer to find a spoon, I saw the rest of the set of knives with A.S. on the handles. I guessed they had belonged to Angus's father, the chef.

Angus stepped into the room "It's better this way. Better than the police taking her." He sat at the table.

"Do you want to tell me exactly what happened?" I asked, knowing he needed to offload.

"When she has a bad phase, Dora runs off and

always ends up there. At the castle." He took a deep breath. "Dora and James were there when the lad fell off."

"They both witnessed it?" I asked.

He nodded. "The doctor said that when she experienced a miscarriage two years ago, it triggered something within her. A deep remorse as Dora blamed herself."

"She didn't…"

He shook his head. "No, it was an accident. The young boy was playing the fool, walking along the wall of the turret, and fell. But Dora blamed herself for allowing him to go with them. As an adult, James used to visit too – to remember the boy. When we were friends, he sometimes spoke of it, when he had been drinking. Both of them were scarred." He looked at me.

"So you had no clue she pushed James off the turret until you read this note from Crow?"

"That day she had gone missing, but as you know I came home. I was here looking for her. Finally, I found her in the woods. She was sitting on the floor singing. I was sure I had found her at three o'clock and as that was the time James died, I presumed it could not possibly have been her. I clearly was wrong. But to think she killed a man and then sat singing afterwards." He shook his head. "My Dora is in there, but a monster has surely clutched her soul." He stopped a sob, took a deep breath and stood up.

"Take your time, Angus," I said.

Prince watched him but was no longer aggressive.

"I've been trying to protect her but now, I can't, not since..."

"What about Simon Crow?"

"I came home from the hotel last night at eleven to find the note on the kitchen table. Dora was out of her room. Edith clearly had not locked the door properly before she left and I could tell Dora had been outside. Her feet were dirty." He stopped to catch his breath.

"Take your time," I said.

"When I asked Dora about the note, she had no recollection of it and it was as if she had read it for the first time. She sobbed uncontrollably." He looked at me. "I think she genuinely did not remember killing James." Angus sniffed. "She said to me, *'what have I done?'* I asked her if she'd seen Simon Crow but she was just repeating, *'it's all my fault,'* which is what she says when she's gone into one of her trances. I took her back to her room and locked the door." He shook his head. "I planned to visit Simon, to plead with him, to explain how Dora was and to hope that because of our history the man would remain quiet." He ran a hand through his hair. "I realised I might have to pay for his silence. But I hoped he would listen."

"So what happened when you got there?" I asked.

Angus let out a sob and slumped to the table. "Sorry." He gulped. "He was dead, stabbed in the stomach. Eyes lifeless, staring up at me. I didn't know what to do. I couldn't believe that Dora had done that to him. My wife, my beautiful Dora, a cold-blooded killer?" He stared at me. "The knife was on the floor and it was from my father's collection. With his initials on." He gestured across the room. "Straight out of my kitchen drawer."

"But what about the slashing and the cross in his inner arm?"

Angus ran a hand through his hair then looked up to the ceiling. "I panicked. The man was already dead, his eyes were staring up at me. I took the knife, slashed off his shirt sleeve and sliced it to resemble a cross." Angus stood up and rushed to his sink and wretched. "S...sorry."

"It's fine, Angus, I used to nurse men in the war." I looked away, taking in the ramifications of the situation – but I was not scared of this man.

Angus drank an entire glass of water and returned to the table. "After that, I took Crow's hat as the trophy, removed the knife and left. I ran up here and buried the evidence in the woods." He sobbed with his head in his hands. "I was trying to protect her." He looked up at me. "With Dora gone, there's no life for me."

"No, Angus, you have the hotel, your father's legacy."

"But I've harboured a criminal, covered up a crime." He shook his head. "If I have to take the blame to protect Dora, I will."

I took a deep breath. "No Angus, she needs to be incarcerated if she kills people. If you take the blame, it may happen again." I knew in my heart that Angus was speaking the truth. That his wife was now out of harm's way. I had never before felt so conflicted. There was the right thing to do, to tell the police, but I did not want to condemn this man who had acted out of love to stage the Vigilante Slasher attack. Who knew what Stone would do to him for tampering with a crime scene. I'd been in enough trouble over a simple scrap of material.

"I have to tell them the truth about what Dora did and what I did," he said.

"In that case, Sergeant Chambers is a very sensible and amiable man. I would avoid speaking to the Inspector from Scotland Yard. He is obsessed with the Slasher. May I suggest you ask Chambers to visit you here?"

He stood up. "Yes, I will face it." He walked out of the kitchen and into the hall and I watched him pick up the receiver of his candlestick telephone. "Please put me through to Branden Bay Police Station," he asked the operator.

Once his call was done, I stood up and approached him. "You are doing the right thing."

I left through the front door with Prince, leaving Angus to wait for Sergeant Chambers.

CHAPTER 18

I felt a deep sadness as I wandered down Castle Road with Prince. Discovering who killed James Millar and Simon Crow had given me no pleasure. I guessed the vision of Dora's innocent and childlike face would haunt me forever, just like the ghost of Lady Astrid of Cleve which supposedly haunted the turret.

As I approached Millar's Hotel, I saw a police car parked outside.

Once inside, I found the reception area empty. I continued past the glass door of the Seaview Restaurant to see the back of a large policeman who I presumed was P.C. Ryan. I stopped and peered around him to see Inspector Stone as he circled the room with his hands clasped behind his back.

Prince barked and Stone spun around and caught my eye. He marched over to the door and pulled it open.

"Come inside." He gestured at me. "Nearly a full house, only Angus Scott is missing. Not at his hotel, unfortunately."

I knew exactly where Angus was but of course did not enlighten the over-eager inspector. I was leaving it up to Angus to give the confession with dignity to Chambers.

"Sit down," Inspector Stone barked in an unpleasant fashion.

Prince snarled at him.

"That mutt needs shooting," he said.

"No," Lottie called from across the room.

I sighed. I really had no energy to suffer the man. I scanned the room to find Camilla, Mrs Flint, Norma, Breckon, Lottie and Thomas. Plus Mary who was seated beside Lottie, scowling across the room at Camilla. Every one of them had a stricken look upon their face. Clearly Inspector Stone was at it again, accusing all and sundry of murder for his own entertainment.

I sauntered past him and sat on the other side of Lottie. Her eyes were red and I guessed she had not heard from Sebastian. I settled Prince down and then took Lottie's hand in mine.

Stone took his position with his hands held behind his back and began to pace. "This was a case fuelled by hate, jealously and family war."

I rolled my eyes, wondering what conclusion the man had arrived at.

He spun around and pointed to Camilla. "A wife

jealous of her husband's indiscretion. You could not forgive him for his affair with Mary O'Malley."

Camilla looked across the room and narrowed her eyes at Mary.

After his somewhat theatrical introduction, he settled into his usual monotone monologue. "You went to India to repair your marriage and that led to disaster."

"I can assure you James loved me and told me he regretted every moment spent with her." Camilla pointed across the room at Mary.

I sighed this whole exercise was completely pointless, given that Angus Scott was confessing to Chambers that Dora had murdered James Millar and Simon Crow. Still, knowing that Stone was about to humiliate himself again, did stop me interrupting.

"So you say, Mrs Millar," Stone said. "You were afraid Mr Millar would divorce you and you would be left with nothing. It would be easier to kill him and profit from the will you believed was in place." He stared at her. "You didn't know he had changed his will only days before his death, did you?"

"No, I did not, but that does not mean I murdered him." She flicked her hair. "And he told me, clearly, that he had made a mistake he intended to rectify." She stared at Thomas who looked wildly around the room.

"So you say," Stone said as he continued to pace the room. "And then we turn to his mistress. Mary O'Malley."

Mary put her hand up. "We were just friends. We

loved each other but James said he would never 'release his burgeoning passion' – they were his exact words – until he divorced Camilla."

"Rubbish, he would never have divorced me." Camilla stood up.

"Mrs Millar, please be quiet," Stone said. "And be seated."

Camilla returned to her chair.

"I know it's hard," Mrs Flint said. "But let the man speak."

Camilla took a deep breath, seemingly realising she should calm her emotions.

"Mary O'Malley was at the crime scene," Stone continued and then faced her. "When you saw James Millar at the castle, you assumed he was there to see you, having admitted that you were waiting for him whilst he took his trip to India."

Mary's lip trembled. "Only because he asked me to."

"I doubt that very much," Norma said, casting a look to Camilla.

Camilla shook her head but made no comment.

Mr Breckon wiped his forehead with a handkerchief. I imagined he'd had quite enough of the goings-on at Millar's Hotel.

"When you saw him at the castle, did you think he was there to meet you?" the Inspector asked Mary.

Tears ran down her cheeks. "Yes."

"So it's possible you become enraged when he told you that you and he had no future. And you pushed him."

"I never spoke to him." Mary took out a handkerchief. "The first time I saw him was after he fell. When he was dead."

"So you say," the Inspector said.

I exchanged a look with Lottie.

"He's read all of this from our notebook," she whispered to me.

"Silence," Stone said to her.

Lottie jumped and I patted her hand. "It doesn't matter, my dear," I whispered. Unable to tell her what I knew whilst Stone was speaking "Please conclude your findings Inspector," I said. "We are extremely weary."

He continued to pace the room. "We are not blessed with Angus Scott's company, but he'd had a deep-rooted hatred of James Millar ever since he built this hotel. And Mr Scott had a torrid affair with Mrs Millar." He shot an accusing look at Camilla.

She sighed and gave a dismissive wave. "It was nothing."

"Scott had gained from the slow demise of your hotel and wanted to ensure it closed forever. But..." He paused. "The real motive lay elsewhere." He stopped and faced Thomas.

"Me?" he said, his face full of fear. For once, the young man appeared completely sober.

"You have the most to benefit from the death."

"That's true," Norma said, nodding towards him.

The Inspector stood before him. "You have inherited an entire hotel." He recommenced his pacing of the room.

"Doesn't mean I killed him," Thomas said.

Stone swung around. "But you are a thief, stealing a precious necklace to raise money – perhaps to pay Crow to murder your uncle before he reverted his will?"

"That's not true," Thomas protested.

"Did you steal a necklace from your uncle?"

Thomas hung his head.

"I knew you stole it," Camilla said as she pointed at her nephew.

"Did you have many discussions in The Branden Arms with Simon Crow?" Inspector Stone asked him.

Thomas said nothing.

Stone continued. "Crow was pressuring you to raise money. Is that true?"

"Yes," Thomas said in a quiet voice. "He said I owed him a large debt."

"For killing your uncle," Stone said with great satisfaction.

Thomas looked up. "No, he said Uncle James owed him."

Stone gestured at him. "You enlisted Crow to do your dirty work and murder your uncle. After failing to sell the necklace to pay his fee, you saw no choice but to kill the man and dress the scene as though it were the work of the Vigilante Slasher." It appeared to me that Stone was laying the blame at Thomas's door.

"That's not true." Thomas stood up and moved away from his chair.

"Ryan," Stone called out.

P.C. Ryan moved forward and Thomas sat back down.

"You would have got away with the murder. But like many criminals, you slipped up. Thinking you were clever – but you're not clever enough." He stared at him.

I knew what was coming, of course.

"You slashed the wrong arm." The Inspector took a deep breath and glanced over at me, I guessed for a reaction.

I stared at him and Stone peered back, realising that I had not been surprised by the revelation of this information. "On the morning of Mr Millar's death, you said..." Stone nodded at Thomas and then opened up his notebook.

Lottie jumped up and called out before Stone could speak. "Thomas, you don't know your left from your right. So it was you, Thomas that killed Crow and pretended it was the work of the Vigilante Slasher." She gave Inspector Stone a rather smug look.

Mrs Flint gasped. "Thomas, how could you!"

"I knew it," Camilla said.

"We said you were a good for nothing lounge lizard," Norma shouted at him.

Breckon gawped at Thomas in disbelief.

Stone's face grew a deep red as if he were going to explode. He was clearly unimpressed that Lottie had stolen his thunder.

Lottie pointed at him. "You got that all that information from our notebook. It's Lady Ellen's work, not yours."

I pulled at Lottie's hand. "Sit down, it really doesn't matter." I knew it made no difference as Thomas was innocent of murder.

Stone spat out his spiel. "I'm arresting you, Thomas Finbarr Jenkins, for the murder of Simon Crow and for solicitation to commit the murder of James Millar."

"I didn't do it," Thomas cried out as he stood with his hands in the air.

P.C. Ryan stepped forward with handcuffs.

"Get away from me," Thomas protested as everyone else gawped at the scene.

I felt I had to say something. "Inspector," I said. "I feel you have the wrong person for this crime."

Stone shot me a look. "Would you care to elaborate, your ladyship?" Sarcasm was dripping off him like candle wax.

I paused. No, I could not. I had left Angus to deal with the confession himself. What if Chambers had been delayed? I remained quiet.

"I didn't think so," Stone said when I failed to answer his question.

The Inspector left the room as Ryan bundled Thomas out. I felt sorry for the young man but knew he would be released once Angus had explained the facts to Chambers.

I looked back to those in the room and in particular the way Camilla, was staring at Mary. I feared an altercation was to follow!

CHAPTER 19

Camilla rose from her chair. "I said from the start it was him."

"I thought he was going to accuse me," Mary said, looking thoroughly relieved.

Camilla spun around to face her. "You can get out now, with your lies about James."

Mary stood up. "I didn't want to come. I went to the police station and the Inspector drove me here. So don't worry, I'm leaving anyway." She pulled her coat from the chair and left.

"I can't believe Thomas would do that to James," Camilla said. Then her face brightened as the news sunk in. "On the plus side, I'm sure I will be successful when I contest the will."

I felt terrible and watched her pull a bottle of champagne from behind the small bar inside the restaurant.

My mouth went dry. "Camilla, I have to inform you. It's not Thomas."

Camilla undid the wire from the bottle. "Let it go, Lady Ellen. The Inspector got it right this time."

"What do you mean, let it go?" I asked. "Thomas is only twenty years old."

"Sounded plausible to me," Mrs Flint said.

"Wouldn't surprise me if he was involved with that Mary," Norma said.

"He's always down The Branden Arms," Lottie added.

Had I not known otherwise, I would have considered it a possibility. Mary was at the castle when James died. Mary was likely at The Branden Arms when Crow was killed.

"Thomas is a thief, he stole the necklace," Camilla said and then popped the cork of the champagne, filling a glass with the frothy liquid.

"Which will get him a few years in gaol, if it was not for the fact that the necklace belongs to him," I said. "You can't sentence a young man to death because you want to make a claim on James's estate."

Camilla paused and narrowed her eyes at me. I could see she longed for the perpetrator to be Thomas.

Mr Breckon got up and hurried out of the room.

"Thomas did it, the evidence is there," Norma said.

"It wasn't him. It was Dora." I hoped Angus had completed his confession. I felt I had to explain. It was unfair for Camilla to think she was going to have a claim on the hotel. However, I rather feared that, even if it had been Thomas, the hotel would have passed to James's sister. But that aside, I felt awful watching Camilla celebrate. I had to break the news to her.

Camilla hesitated. I'd clearly caught her attention. She looked annoyed but I could tell she was curious. I kept my gaze fixed upon her.

Camilla sighed as she picked up her glass. "Are you sure?"

"Positive. Angus has had Dora committed," I said, relieved that she appeared to believe me.

"Oh no," Mrs Flint said. "Dora was always a troubled soul." She put a hand to her chest. "To think she killed her childhood friend."

Camilla walked across the room and placed her glass on a table before slumping to a chair. "Dora killed James?"

I nodded. "I'm afraid so."

"So who killed Crow?" Lottie asked.

"Dora." I held back the part about it being Angus that staged the Slasher attack hoping that Chambers may have found a way to protect him.

Camilla downed her glass of champagne. "Dora was not of sane mind. Angus kept her locked up for a reason." She stood up and sighed. "The dream was good while it lasted. I thought the hotel was mine. At least I've already packed."

"I'm so sorry, Camilla," I said. "I know you would have been relieved thinking it was Thomas. It's not what you want to hear."

"I'm going back to the room," Lottie said.

"I'll join you," I said. I needed to change my clothes.

215

"I called him a lounge lizard to his face," Norma mumbled to Mrs Flint as we left the room. "He'll chuck us out as soon as he's back."

"He still stole that necklace though. They might keep him in for a while," Mrs Flint said.

Once we were in the suite, Lottie helped me change out of my dishevelled clothing as I brought her up to date.

"Oh my goodness," Lottie said.

"You should have seen Dora Scott up close, with her hair and skin so white, it's clear why everyone thought she was a ghost."

"So she pushed James over the edge?"

"It appears so."

Once dressed I left Lottie with Prince, deciding to go downstairs and wait for Hamilton to tell him the news once he returned from Bristol.

As I passed the Seaview Restaurant, Camilla called me in. She had also changed clothes and pulled a nearly empty bottle of champagne from the bar. "Mrs Flint is packing my final pieces. I just can't face doing it myself. I'm saying a goodbye toast to the hotel and to James."

She topped her glass up with the bubbly liquid as I heard the evening rain batter the large windows.

We sat in silence for a while. My stomach burned and I sighed. "I still can't believe such a frail woman killed Simon Crow. How did she manage it?"

"Crow was a womaniser but he didn't have any love unless he paid for it," Camilla said. "Apart from his unfortunate looks, he probably considered falling in love to be a weakness."

"So you think she seduced him?" I asked, my eyes wide open, thinking of the sweet-looking Dora.

"Easily done with that man," Camilla said with a short laugh. "But Inspector Stone's a fool thinking it was Thomas. I would have thought having Angus's initials engraved on the knife would have sent them to his house a lot sooner." She slurred. "Maybe he thought the Slasher had the same initials? Andrew Symes, Albert Shrewsbury, the man has probably been scouring the Southwest." She stopped then looked at me.

I sat processing what she had said as a chill entered my bones. I had not mentioned the initials on the knife to anyone. Only Angus Scott, myself and the killer would know that. My face felt hot as my heartbeat quickened. I dragged my gaze away from Camilla as Mrs Flint came to the door.

"Camilla. John's put your bags and trunk in the car. It's all set for the morning." Mrs Flint gave a sad smile. "I'm off to bed, I'll be up early to see you off."

I heard the words I had spoken in my head and written in my notebook. *We will have to wait for the killer to slip up.* I felt as if I was falling down a rabbit hole. Not only had Inspector Stone been wrong, so had I! I stood up. "I'm shattered. But I can't go to bed until I know Hamilton is back. His train should be in soon. I think I'll collect Lottie and Prince and take a slow walk to the station. Even if the weather is dreadful, I'm in need of some fresh air."

Camilla stared at me over the top of her champagne. "It's raining, I'll drive you." She placed her glass on the table and stood up.

"Is your head clear enough?" I asked. "With all the champagne you've had?"

"I drive much better after a few drinks." Camilla laughed, suddenly appearing more alert. "Come along." She picked up a large handbag.

I guessed it was the easiest way to get her into town and closer to the police station. I did not want to leave Lottie with her. The fog that had hung over me, thinking how unbelievable it was that Dora was a killer, was clearing. I should have trusted my gut instinct. I had felt bad about Dora being responsible for murder for a good reason – she was innocent.

Camilla walked ahead through the empty reception area.

I slowed down, hoping that Hamilton would walk through the door at any moment.

"Oh, I haven't got my coat," I said.

Camilla waved her hand. "You don't need it. I'm driving and the car is under the canopy."

"Oh yes," I said as I followed her outside into the damp chilly night. My body trembled and my mouth felt dry. I was getting into the motorcar of a killer. I had to remain cool and calm so I did not raise her suspicion.

"You'll have to sit in the back," she said when we

reached the car. "The trunk is on the front seat and I won't be able to move it.

I climbed in behind the passenger seat, as Camilla sat at the front. The glass window between the driving seat and the back was already open. Apart from one rear passenger seat, the car was full. As Camilla placed her bag next to her, I glimpsed the purple pouch James Millar's necklace was kept in. This was clearly how she intended to finance herself whilst she sought a new life.

"Where are you going to move to?" I asked, trying to sound breezy and not let her know she had slipped up by mentioning the initials on the knife when I had not told anyone about them. I guessed that Camilla had been the one to seduce and kill Simon Crow. She was confident that it would be easy to overpower the man because that's exactly what she had done herself.

"I'll tour the south coast and make contacts. Then settle somewhere and start again," Camilla said.

As we set off, a taxicab approached the hotel. In the back was Hamilton.

"Hamilton is here," I said to Camilla with relief.

She ignored me and continued to drive.

I put my hand on the glass as Hamilton passed. I caught his eye and mouthed 'help'.

Hamilton frowned then tapped the driver on the shoulder as Camilla sped away.

"Stop, Camilla." I said. "Hamilton is here. I don't need to go to the station."

She remained silent and carried on as the rain

battered the windscreen. I was under no illusion – Camilla knew she'd slipped up.

"Camilla," I said louder from the backseat. "You're just making it worse."

She turned the car as we reached Beach Road with a squeak of the wheels and sped up. "No one will know unless you tell them." She cranked the windscreen wiper as the car swerved and she dodged an onward coming car.

I held onto the side of the car as she pelted along.

"I'm not stupid," she said. "I saw a change in you. What was it?"

There was no point denying it. "It was the knife. I've not mentioned the initials on it to anyone. Only the killer would have known that. The knife was not left at the scene. Angus removed it."

"Of course. I guessed Angus had covered it up once everyone mentioned the Slasher. It's obvious he would not have left the knife. That's tiredness and champagne for you. So inventive of him dressing it up as a Slasher attack." She turned around and looked at me, swerving. "And how clever, yet again the esteemed Lady Ellen solves a mystery." She faced front and steadied the car again, heading for the road out of town.

I needed to slow her down so leaned forward to discuss the murder. "When James arranged to meet someone at three o'clock, you didn't know where he was off to so followed him, didn't you? You disguised yourself taking a brown overcoat and hat belonging to one of the hotel guests." My mind flashed back to the man leaving the hotel, complaining that he did not have his hat and coat.

Camilla made no comment and again cleared the rain from the screen.

"You knew your marriage was over, you wanted to know James's plans. Wondering where he was going and more importantly who he was meeting."

"I think a wife is allowed to follow her husband when he has cheated on her!" Camilla called out.

"You found he was going to the castle and thought he was there to meet Mary. You followed him up the turret, argued with him and pushed him off. All that talk about him realising he had made a big mistake and you were the only one for him was one big lie." I steadied myself as Camilla took a sharp bend.

"We always made up after a falling out." She accelerated as the road straightened.

"Not his time. You knew he was going to divorce you. So you killed him, believing you would inherit the hotel as per the original will."

"Shut up!" Camilla screeched at me but she slowed a little.

"Knowing you would get more than if he divorced you. But what you didn't know was that he had already seen the solicitor."

Camilla slowed then pulled onto the Bristol Road.

"Probably hot in that overcoat, you discarded it in the priest hole and then ripped your blouse escaping from the tunnel to the woods. But you kept the hat on to disguise your hair. I presume you threw the blouse away when you reached home. How did you achieve that without getting noticed?"

"I helped design the hotel, there are many concealed entrances." Camilla slowed a little as she spoke. "But no-one saw me. Once inside I disposed of my entire uniform and took a bath where I stayed until I received the awful news." It was as if she relished telling me how clever she had been.

"You thought you'd got away with it until you found the note from Crow, saying he witnessed you killing James and to meet him."

"The man was revolting and won't be missed." Her voice was steady.

I battled to keep my voice steady. Engaging her in conversation was slowing her down and it would give Hamilton a chance to catch us up. I looked behind. It was difficult to see clearly out of the rain drenched window. But there was no sign of any lights and fear gripped my heart. He must have taken a different turn.

I turned back to the front. "When you received the letter from Crow, you must have realised it was actually Crow who had arranged to meet James. Your husband wasn't there to see Mary at all."

Camilla slowed down even more. My tactic was working.

"Did you see Dora in the woods?" I asked.

"I heard the stupid woman singing as I escaped. I knew she often went on a walkabout to the castle. Angus had confided in me."

"Framing Dora was a genius plan," I said, complimenting her. "How did you get into their house?"

"I've known Angus for years. I knew where the spare door key was. I went in the front and opened the bedroom where he locks up the animal he calls his wife. I hid whilst she went out the back door, then when the coast was clear, took the knife with his father's initials on. I left the letter I had received from Crow on the kitchen table with an opened envelope upon which I wrote *Dora Scott*. As if she'd opened it and left it. I shut the front door and replaced the key under the plant pot."

The more she talked, the slower she drove.

"That was an excellent plan. And then you killed Crow?"

"It was easy. I didn't have to do much for Simon to think it was his lucky night. He closed his eyes and I pulled the knife from my bag and that was it. I stepped back and waited. It wasn't long until he died."

"What you really wanted was Angus Scott to find the note and call the police who would find the body and his knife beside it. And then he would think his wife was a monster and Dora would go to prison, leaving you with the option of rekindling your friendship with Angus. By then you knew Thomas had inherited Millar's, so why not go for The Grand?"

"Dora won't hang and he locked her up anyway, at home."

"What you didn't bank on was Angus finding Crow's body, then trying to pass the murder off as a

Vigilante Slasher attack to protect the woman he loves."

"He didn't want bad publicity for the hotel. He doesn't love her! Angus always adored me. We were with each other every day at The Grand, until that imp turned up." She put her foot down, speeding up. Getting her thinking and talking slowed her down but angering her had the opposite effect. "If it wasn't for her, I would still be at The Grand with Angus and wouldn't have bothered with James at all. He was never the man Angus is."

I held on to the door handle. I was preparing myself to open it and jump out as soon as she slowed, because every time I looked out of the back window there was no sign of car headlamps on the road behind us.

Camilla screeched the car to a stop and then drove through a gate into a field. We bumped up and down until she reached the edge where trees lined it. She slammed on the brakes and I lurched forward.

"And this is where it all ends," Camilla said leaving the engine to tick over. "I'll be saying goodbye to you here and be on my way to a new life."

I relaxed. It would be a long way back but I was fit enough to walk a few miles. Even if I would be drenched. I reached for the car door handle.

"But I can't afford to let you live." She pulled a knife from her bag.

"No!" I said as she pulled her arm back. I pushed myself back and heard the sound of a motorcar. Turning around, I saw it bouncing across the grass at speed. I knew it must be Hamilton. Just as I was going to open the door, Camilla put the car into gear and put her foot down, reversing then turning right. The car was not gaining speed as fast as the car hurtling towards us. I leaned across the seat diagonally and grabbed hold of her shoulder and pushed her, trying to reach the steering wheel.

"Get off me," she screamed and as she lashed out, she lost control of the car. I had enough time to brace myself for the crash as bushes seemed to come up towards us in slow motion. Camilla's cry stopped when the car came to a halt with a thud.

The engine had cut out and I heard a hiss from the bonnet. I fumbled for the handle of the door but it was soon yanked open by Hamilton.

Camilla groaned from the seat in front of me, her head having hit the steering wheel.

"Ellen," Hamilton said as he took me in his arms.

I took a deep breath. "I didn't realise you had followed us. I thought…" I trailed off but was deter-mined not to descend into tears.

"The driver had turned the headlamps off. We'd been gaining on you when we saw her turn off the road."

The driver joined us. "Shall we check on her?" He pointed to a groaning Camilla.

"Be careful, she's a knife in there. And she killed both James Millar and Simon Crow."

The driver walked carefully to check on Camilla.

I lowered my voice. "Angus Scott found Crow's

body and tampered with the scene to make it look as though the Vigilante Slasher did it. He wanted to protect his wife because Camilla had set it up to look like Dora was the killer."

"Well done Ellen, you are a most remarkable sleuth."

My head thumped as Hamilton helped me to the taxicab. Then returned with the driver for Camilla.

CHAPTER 20

I woke feeling refreshed. It was two days since we had delivered Camilla to Branden Bay Police Station and then spent the rest of the night giving full statements. Inspector Stone had left for Bristol that night before we had even arrived and Chambers had not heard from him since. The very day we had delivered Camilla to the police station, the Vigilante Slasher had struck again in Bristol. It was Donny Fingo's brother Larry who was the victim this time. His cigar was taken as a trophy. I assumed that was keeping Inspector Stone busy and he was unlikely to want to show his face, considering they had to release Thomas. With Camilla in custody, it appeared that Chambers had struck Angus Scott's confession to tampering with the crime scene from the records as his involvement was never mentioned again. Gossip and the newspapers claimed that Camilla was responsible for mimicking the Slasher attack.

Since that fateful day, I had spent the entire time in my suite. The only person I had seen had been Lottie. We had remained at Millar's hotel. Thomas had been so grateful to us for discovering the real killer. The police had released him for stealing the necklace, considering it was his own property. Lottie had told me that the young man had changed his tune and had been shocked into looking at life through different eyes, having been convinced he was destined for the gallows.

I entered the main living area of the suite to be met by Lottie as she stormed into the room in floods of tears.

"Whatever's the matter?" I asked as she stood before me with a tear-stained face and a letter clutched in her hand.

Prince whimpered as he looked up at her.

"Sebastian's gone to Ireland to spend two months there before university. His parents have insisted on it."

"You've been apart for longer than that in the past. The pain is only worse as you've seen more of him recently."

"It's not the time he's spending away from me. Ireland is where the girl lives that he's supposed to marry."

I took a step backwards. "He's engaged?" I asked. *No wonder his mother was so livid,* I thought.

"It's not official. The parents decided they should wed. He's not even seen her since he was eleven."

I breathed out. At least he had not been betrothed.

"Sebastian is his own man. I doubt he'll succumb to a forced marriage but as I said, a relationship with him long-term is unlikely."

Lottie pulled a handkerchief from her sleeve and wiped her eyes. "I know that, Ellen. But when we're together, it seems perfect, like it's truly meant to be."

I moved forward and hugged her. "I'm sure he will write again soon and tell you how he is hating every minute, that the girl he is supposed to marry is dull and that he can't wait to see you again."

She sniffed as Prince sat at her feet. "He did say that I'm the only girl for him and he'll dream of me every night."

"There you go, you have nothing to worry about for now. But when you next see him, you must have a serious talk about the future."

She nodded. "I know."

I left Lottie in the room, writing to Sebastian who had given her the address of a post office where he would pick up his mail.

When I reached the reception desk with Prince at heel, Thomas was looking through a pile of papers.

"You seem engrossed," I said.

"I'm trying to understand all of this," he said.

"I hear you are going to stay at the hotel?"

He nodded. "I telegrammed my parents and they're leaving India. My inheritance is going to be released early and we're going to build the spa that Uncle James wanted. Then reopen next spring, assuming the work has been completed."

"You seem like a different man," I said to him.

"I haven't drunk anything since my arrest," he said. "I feel as if I've been given a new chance. And everyone's being so good to me. Mary O'Malley is starting back here tomorrow."

"I'm sure she will be a great help to you," I said with a smile.

"There you are," Hamilton called out.

I spun around and Prince greeted him with his tail wagging.

He approached me. "I thought you'd gone into hibernation."

I laughed. "I needed the rest. It's been quite a turbulent few weeks. When does your new job start?"

"In one week. I'm hoping to spend at least some time relaxing here before I go but I'm rather scared to mention it too loudly."

I laughed. "I know what you mean. Is there anything you have in mind?"

"Reading outside in the hotel gardens, watching the sea come in and go out. With perhaps a sunset walk along the beach."

Prince barked eagerly.

"That sounds perfect. Do you mind me tagging along every now and again?"

"Ellen, I'd be delighted." He offered me his arm. "I'm going for a stroll now, if you would care to join me?"

* * *

I HAD ENJOYED a wonderful and relaxing week with Hamilton and Lottie. Lottie was not as joyful as usual and I knew that she was missing Sebastian. With no excitement to take her mind off his absence, I felt powerless to cheer her up.

It was soon time to bid Hamilton farewell.

"Would you like us to walk you to the station?" I asked.

He shook his head. "My new employer is sending a motorcar."

"Travelling in style?" I asked with a laugh.

"I hope so. You have the address?" Hamilton asked.

"Yes and I will write, keeping you up to date with our daily life."

"Stay out of trouble," he said to Lottie and me with a laugh.

Ten minutes later, we waved as he drove away in an extremely smart red motorcar.

"I'm taking Prince for a walk," Lottie said.

"I will start the packing. We cannot stay at Millar's any longer." I was certainly ready for a change of scenery.

Mrs Flint, Norma and Mr Breckon had been keeping the empty hotel maintained and helping Thomas plan for his future. I knew he would ensure they would be able to retain their employment with him. The three were set for a week's break, accompanied by Mr Flint, to the south coast to watch Joseph in his travelling show. They wanted a break before returning to the hotel to welcome Thomas's parents. I took this as an ideal moment for us to move on from Millar's Hotel.

I had spoken to Angus the week before and arranged a suite. I had also passed him details of a doctor who had visited Ashcombe Hall many times helping soldiers that suffered with shell-shock. I thought it would be useful for Dora. Angus was determined to ensure she returned home and said that rather than leaving her locked up in her bedroom, he would never leave her out of his sight again. Instead he planned to take her to the hotel, to integrate her back into the real world instead of trying to hide her from it.

After Lottie and Prince had left, I walked back inside.

"Your newspaper is here, my lady," Mary said, handing me a letter along with it. She had already settled in.

"Thank you," I said.

I took the paper and letter upstairs. The letter was from a friend of mine from school. I had written to her about my adventures in Branden Bay and she had invited me to stay with her for a proper rest. It wasn't that far from where Hamilton would be in Dulverton. Did I really want to visit her? Or was it the possibility of being able to see Hamilton making the trip more appealing than it would otherwise be?

I looked out over the sea, realising I was missing him already. Then I thought of Lottie and how she felt about Sebastian. I decided that, as nice as Branden Bay was, a change of scenery for us both would be in order.

Even if it was for a couple of weeks. I decided to write to Lady Denham and accept her invitation, as well as advising her that I would be accompanied by Lottie and Prince. We would spend one week at The Grand Hotel before leaving town.

After writing the letter which I intended to post that same day, I pulled the newspaper from the table. The headings were still covering the Vigilante Slasher's attack in Bristol. I turned the pages, having no wish to read any more about the man. I stopped and took a sharp intake of breath. There was a photograph of Sebastian and next to him was one of the most beautiful and glamorous women I had ever set eyes on. Tall elegant with thick dark hair.

Engagement Announcement

The Marquis and Marchioness of Bandberry are delighted to announce the engagement of their son Sebastian Henry, Earl of Garthorn to Lady Clara Victoria O'Connor, daughter of the Duke and Duchess of Derrylake. The engaged couple have been acquainted since childhood and their families are overjoyed with their news. The wedding is not expected for some years as the Earl of Garthorn is reading English at Oxford University.

Underneath was an editorial comment:

High Society celebrates the union of these esteemed families and will no doubt follow their engagement with interest and look forward to what promises to be the wedding of the decade.

I closed the newspaper. How on earth would Lottie react? I sighed. Clearly Sebastian *had* succumbed to the wishes of his family and I was not surprised. I expected Sebastian to write to Lottie and explain the situation and decided it would be better to wait until she heard from him, rather than read about it in the newspaper.

"Poor Lottie," I said to myself as I deposited the newspaper into the waste paper basket. I decided to ask Mary to forward on any mail for us and wait for the difficult news to be received, at which time I would strive to be the best sister Lottie could have. I knew for sure, in spite of our differing stations, that was how I regarded her.

IS SEBASTIAN REALLY ENGAGED? Catch up with Ellen and Lottie when Hamilton invites them for a day at Moor House in Dulverton. A priceless artefact is stolen and the owner asks Ellen and Lottie to stay and help Hamilton find the thief! Order *A Mystery at Moor House.*

IF YOU WOULD LIKE to read the prequel and find out how Ellen met Hamilton and rescued Prince from a fate many runts faced join my newsletter at www. subscribepage.io/Kellysnews

ACKNOWLEDGMENTS

I'd like to thank my creative writing tutor Rosemary Dun, both inside the OU and out! You encouraged me to pursue novel writing and gave me so much information and guidance, I'm still reading the handouts! You are amazing. Thanks also goes to my brilliant mentors Alison Knight and Jenny Kane of Imagine Creative Writing and their Novel in a Year course, which gave me lots of help and kept me on track.

Thanks to the inspirational friends I met through the Romantic Novelists' Association, and the Bristol writing community (I'm too scared to list everyone in case I miss someone off!) And to my Beta readers, Tara Starling, Cinnomen Matthews McGuigan, Michelle Armitage, Tara Starling, Shell Rice Mortimer and Leanne Goodall. Thanks also to Helen Blenkinsop who is a guru on the 'hook' and amazon ads. And thanks to my best writing friends – Callie Hill, Claire O'Conner and Jenny Treasure, for also being beta readers and for sharing the journey with me. And to my Women's Fic mastermind and my accountability partner Soraya. My Editor Becky Halls. And not forgetting my two author mates, Laura and Andy who make life fun!

Thank you to my advance reader team who are

really supportive and there for me, even from the first book.

Thank you to those on my mailing list who interact with me.

Thanks to my family for supporting me, especially Gary for putting up with me tapping away at the keyboard 24/7.

Printed in Great Britain
by Amazon

52327467R00138